A Match Made by Chloe

t.b. pearl

Have enough courage to trust love one more time. And always one more time.

~ Maya Angelou

ONE

———

Chloe Daniels was running late. Again. As always.

It was bad enough when she was late in meeting her best friend, Jenna, for dinner or when picking up her visiting mother from the airport. But it was ten times worse when she was meeting a potential client for the first time. Especially that day's potential client, Brad Maylis, the Yankees' all-star pitcher.

As the taxi pulled up to the entrance of a corner coffee shop in the West Village, Chloe tossed a twenty in the direction of the driver's seat and dashed out of the cab to the front door of the shop, which was abuzz with a flux of patrons desperately in need of coffee. She paused at the door, smoothed down the front of her skirt and took a calming breath. Then she entered in search of her client.

He had told her he would be wearing a black Atlanta Braves cap low over his eyes – as much of a disguise as Brad would permit himself. It did not take her long to scope out the hat in a sea of suits, ties and high-heeled boots. He was lounging at a corner table, sipping a grandé and reading a book. A mystery novel to be exact.

Chloe smiled at the fact that he was not reading the *New York Metro's* sports section or the recent edition of *NY Woman*, which had crowned him the City's most eligible bachelor. Chloe had read the story days before she got the call from Brad himself that he was looking for love and wanted to hire her as a matchmaker. She later chuckled at the irony that the editors at *NY Woman* had no idea their Mr. Most Eligible was not only looking for love, he was ready to settle down.

"Sorry I'm late," Chloe said upon approach.

"No worries." Brad smiled up at her, a smile of lazy confidence, of a warm and happy upbringing in a small town in Tennessee. Coupled with a pair of hazel eyes that contrasted quite sexily with his tanned complexion, Chloe could easily understand why the editors at *NY Woman* were so smitten.

He moved to stand. "You want something to drink?"

"Oh no, I'm good. Thank you," she replied, sitting across from him.

"You sure? The coffee here's really good."

"Really? I'll have to get some on the way out."

"You must be a morning person."

"Kind of. Why?"

"I can't put two words together without a cup o' Joe."

She smiled at that.

"But I gotta say, Ms. Daniels, I've been looking forward to this meeting all week."

"Please, call me Chloe."

"When my buddy Clark told me about you, I was like, man, you gotta hook me up."

Chloe's face brightened. "Clark and Annie. How are they doing?"

Clark, a baseball scout, and Annie, an antiquities professor, were one of her first matches when she took a leap of faith, quit her job and began matchmaking full-time.

"They're good," Brad replied. "They're expecting baby number two any day now."

"No way!"

"And they can't sing your praises enough."

"Oh I'm so happy for them. Please tell them I said congratulations the next time you see them."

"You got it," he replied, that lazy grin of his making an appearance once more.

"So why do you think you need a matchmaker? Is it because of your busy schedule?"

Chloe had worked with a few professional athletes thus far and she knew that, despite their celebrity, the game and its lifestyle made dating and relationships difficult.

She also asked certain preliminary questions to make sure a person was truly ready for love. She never officially took on a client unless they were ready. And she found it was best to screen a potential client in-person, so she could gage their body language. Hence this early-morning meeting at Brad's favorite coffee shop.

Brad leaned forward, resting his arms on the table and wrapping his hands around the coffee cup. "Actually, it's because of my parents. They met through a local matchmaker back home in Tennessee…"

"Really!" Chloe's face brightened even more. Rarely did she meet someone who was the product of a matchmaker.

Brad nodded. "Mrs. Lucille. She didn't have a matchmaking business or anything, she was just a cashier at the grocery store; the only grocery store in town. So she knew pretty much everybody. And every now and again, she'd be talking to a customer, then out of the blue she'd say, 'you know what, I know someone who'd be perfect for you.' That's exactly what happened to my dad. One minute he's chewing the fat with Mrs. Lucille about heirloom tomatoes; the next, she's telling him there's a lady she wants him to meet."

"Your mom?"

"Yep. And my parents have been together ever since. Forty-three years."

"That's so awesome," she said with a grin. "So… why now?"

"Why now?" he said, gazing pensively into the coffee cup, giving the question the serious thought it deserved. "I'm just ready."

He looked up, his eyes connecting with hers. "I've

actually been ready the past two years, I just haven't met the right woman yet."

Chloe nodded, that was often the case with men. Some just woke up one day, ready for marriage. While others only got the marriage itch once they met the woman of their dreams, at which point they immediately started strategizing when and where to propose.

Chloe studied Brad's eyes and his body language as he continued.

"Honestly, when it comes down to it, I just want what my parents have – a lover, a best friend, a family..."

As he spoke, Chloe noted how relaxed his body was, his eyes unwavering and sincere. Before her sat a man who knew what he wanted and meant what he said.

"I think there's something really special about being able to build a life with someone you love," he continued.

A man who had just become her newest client!

Chloe's lips parted into a luminous grin.

"What? Too sappy?" Brad asked.

"Not at all. In fact, it's exiting."

"How's that?" he said, his eyes filling with curiosity.

"Because I can't wait to help you find what you've been searching for."

Brad smiled back at her as though she were Santa Claus, the Tooth Fairy and the Easter Bunny all wrapped into one. Chloe was always blown away when a client truly believed in her gift as a matchmaker. Granted, since all of her clients were by referral only, they were almost always referred by someone whose marriage or relationship was a product of her matchmaking.

Yet, it was one thing for someone to tell you that a matchmaker is the *real deal*, and quite another to blindly believe it yourself. Most of her clients came to her with a glimmer of hope that she would live up to her reputation, but they were prepared to be disappointed just in case.

Very few came to her with the blind faith she saw in Brad's eyes. And while she always gave her clients two-hundred percent, it was for clients like Brad that she would scour to the ends of the Earth in search of their soulmate.

Time, money and self-preservation be damned.

"But before we get started, I'm curious... is Mrs. Lucille still alive?" Chloe asked.

She had yet to meet another true-blue matchmaker who was gifted like herself, and was secretly hoping Mrs. Lucille could be her first. It would be akin to meeting an elder artisan; a fount of wisdom who had mastered a craft Chloe had just begun to practice in an official capacity.

"Oh no, she passed, hell, about ten years back," Brad replied.

Chloe's heart sank. *Alas.*

"But she lived a good long life. Ninety-eight years."

"Wow."

"And she was matching people up even on her death bed."

Chloe smiled. She wondered if she would go out the same way.

"So how did she go about introducing your mom to your dad?"

Brad chuckled. "Well, it wasn't a hop, skip and a jump, I can tell you that. My mom was engaged to someone at the time, so Mrs. Lucille's first order of business was finding a way to break them up..."

"You're joking!"

"Hand on the Bible; I kid you not. But Farrow was, and still is, a small town. Back then, you couldn't sneeze without a dozen people calling you to say, 'achoo.' So Mrs. Lucille had to figure out a way to break off the engagement without anyone knowing she was pulling the strings…"

As Brad spoke, a thin thread, invisible to everyone but her, suddenly looped around his shoulders. The thread was pink in hue and shimmered as though it was comprised of thousands of miniature diamonds.

Chloe blinked.

Then blinked again.

Then she blinked once more to ensure her eyes were not deceiving her.

Sure enough, the thread she had long-ago christened, *the thread of kismet*, remained looped around her new client.

This is definitely a first, Chloe thought, completely in awe of Serendipity.

She turned her head to the right and followed the thread, which had looped around a woman in her early thirties. The woman was dressed in a power suit and *fierce* heels, with a bang swept across her forehead and her jet black hair pulled back into an over-the-shoulder ponytail. She was typing a message on her cell phone as she stood fifth in line from the counter.

Chloe's entire demeanor shifted as she became laser-focused on the woman in the power suit. Her pupils dilated, her heart quickened and the noise in the shop faded away.

First things first, Chloe thought, her gaze zeroing in on the woman's ring finger, which was wonderfully bare.

Yes!

But her elation was short-lived because, as Chloe knew all too well, just because a person was unmarried, did not mean they were unattached. Hard as it was for her to do, she always refrained from connecting soulmates when one of them was in a relationship. She took it as a sign that it was not the right time for said soulmates to meet.

Chloe's demeanor shifted once more as she began to strategize a plan of action. The quickest way for her to discover the woman's relationship status was to ask her directly. Which meant Chloe had to figure out the best way to approach a woman who did not know her from Eve, and ask her if she was single and looking for love – without coming across as weird... or flirtatious... or a snake oil salesman.

So focused was Chloe on her target that she barely heard Brad's voice above the fog of her own thoughts. It took a second for her to register that he had asked if she was okay.

"Yes, uh..."

She forced herself to pry her gaze from the woman and back to Brad.

"I'm sorry. I think..."

Chloe hesitated. She hated lying as much as she loathed liars. But she needed a plausible reason to excuse herself from the table without rousing Brad's suspicion or, worse, questions about her sanity.

"I just saw someone I went to college with. Someone I haven't seen in years," she said.

"Small world, eh?"

"Indeed."

Chloe turned her head to the right once more. She glanced briefly at the woman, who was now third in line from the cashier, before resting her gaze on the front door – hoping to lead Brad to believe that her 'old friend' had just exited the shop.

"I hate to do this but, would you excuse me for a moment?" she asked.

Brad nodded. "Sure. Take your time."

Chloe smiled to herself. That was one of the many things she loved about Southerners; they were rarely in much of any hurry.

Chloe stood outside the coffee shop, waiting for the woman to emerge.

As she did so, she mentally donned her sales cap. Sensing someone's soulmate, that was easy. Approaching them and persuading them to go on a blind date, that was the tricky part. Thankfully, she had a few techniques to draw upon from her days as a business consultant, wherein it was her job to land and keep Fortune 500 clients.

The door to the shop jingled and her target emerged with a mocha latte in hand. Chloe's senses shifted into overdrive as she watched the woman pivot in the direction of a nearby subway entrance.

"Excuse me, miss," Chloe said, following after her. "Miss..."

The woman stopped and turned.

"Sorry to bother you," Chloe continued. "I was hoping you wouldn't mind..."

"I hate to cut you off, but I'm kinda in a hurry," the woman said kindly but not too kindly, girding herself against unwanted solicitation – as any true-blue New Yorker would do.

"I understand. And I promise this won't take more than a minute of your time. It's a quick 3-question survey on love."

After months of trial and error, Chloe had found that this line almost always worked – simultaneously piquing a person's interest while putting them somewhat at ease.

"Okay," the woman replied, her eyes alighting with curiosity.

"What's your name?"

"Lia."

Chloe reached out to shake her hand. "Nice to meet you Lia. I'm Chloe. Okay, so first question..." she said, starting with the most important question of all. "Are you single or in a relationship?"

Chloe held her breath, hoping, wishing, praying that Lia's response would be:

"I'm single," Lia replied. "Woefully single," she added with a sigh.

Chloe's heart smiled. *Not for much longer.*

"Do you believe in soulmates?"

"I don't know... I'd... like to."

"What if I told you that I'm a professional matchmaker and I know someone who is perfect for you?"

A shadow fell over Lia's face. "I'd say, what's the catch and how much?"

"No catch," Chloe said, smiling reassuringly. "And it'll only cost you a little bit of your time and an open mind."

Upon hearing those last two words, Lia frowned. "Is he cute?" she asked.

You have no idea.

"Oh, he's very, very cute," Chloe replied.

Lia then asked the question most women ask after gauging a man's attractiveness.

"What does he do?"

Chloe hesitated. She definitely could not reveal that Lia's mystery man was a professional baseball player. That was something only Brad could divulge, if he felt comfortable doing so on their first date.

"He... works in sports marketing."

Lia nodded, taking this in.

———

Chloe reached into her purse and pulled out a business card. "I'd love to set you two up on a blind date."

She handed the card to Lia.

"Think about it and if you're interested, give me a call and let me know your availability this weekend or the next," Chloe added, creating just a hint of urgency.

"Okay, thanks," Lia said solemnly, studying the card.

"Enjoy the rest of your day," Chloe said as Lia continued on towards the subway.

From her days as a corporate consultant, Chloe had learned the art of the sell; and the importance of knowing when to hard sell and when to soft sell. While the hard sell had been an effective tool in the corporate world, when it came to professional matchmaking, she found that she did indeed attract more bees with honey.

The key to success for anyone in the business of people was learning to put oneself in the customers' shoes. Chloe understood that trusting a total stranger to set you up on a blind date with your supposed soulmate was a tall order. And she respected that some people needed time and space to think things through and decide if they were willing to take such a leap of faith.

I really, really hope she calls, Chloe thought as she approached the door to the coffee shop.

And on the off-chance Lia did not call – that she ended up getting cold feet; or meeting a handsome stranger during happy hour that night; or quitting her high-powered job on a whim to cross 'trekked the Himalayas' off her bucket list – Chloe would have to accept the fact that Brad and Lia were meant to meet at a different time, under different circumstances.

She had long ago realized it was futile to tempt or argue with Fate.

"Actually..." came the sound of Lia's voice from behind. Chloe turned to see Lia walking back towards her.

"I'm in," she said with a smile, her eyes filled with anticipation.

Hallelujah!

"Great!" Chloe replied, barely able to contain her glee.

"I'm out of town this weekend, but next weekend I'm totally available."

Chloe gave an enthusiastic nod. "I'll try to set something up for next weekend."

She already had an idea where she would have them meet. Since Brad was a high-profile client and a darling of the paparazzi – especially when it came to his dating life – his blind date would need to occur at a place that was private and off-the-beaten path, yet still romantic.

She had a former client whose parents owned a botanical garden on Long Island that was only available for private tours and events. The parents were always thrilled to help when Chloe called for a favor, since they credited her for gifting them with two adorable grandchildren... by way of helping their son find his soulmate four years before.

"Here's my card," Lia said, handing Chloe a business card with the insignia of a well-known Fortune 500 – one of Chloe's former corporate clients, in fact.

"Perfect," she replied, grinning from ear to ear. "I'll be in touch."

"I'm looking forward to it," Lia said, waving in farewell.

Chloe watched as Lia made her way down the

block to the subway entrance; the thread of kismet slowly fading from view.

Chloe re-entered the coffee shop and navigated her way through the line of patrons back to Brad, who was engrossed, once more, in the mystery novel.

"Hi," she said, her face aglow.

Brad looked up. "Looks like you had a memorable reunion."

"Actually," she began, sitting down, "I have a confession to make."

Brad cocked his head. "Okay…"

"What I said earlier about seeing an old friend from college, it was a lie."

Brad furrowed his brow. Chloe could imagine he was trying to grasp why she would fib about something so inane.

"I'm truly sorry about that. Lying is something I never really do. But it was for a good cause. A *great* cause in fact!"

Brad stared back at her, awaiting the punch line.

"Are you free next Saturday or Sunday?" she asked.

"I should be, next Sunday at least. Why?"

Chloe grinned. "So I can introduce you to your soulmate."

Brad blinked. "You think you'll find her that soon?"

"I just did," she gushed, still in disbelief herself.

"What, you mean in here?"

Chloe nodded.

Brad leaned back in his seat, as though a baseball had just slammed into his chest. "Well I'll be. So that's why you went outside."

"Again, I'm so sorry about the little white lie."

Brad's lips widened into the sexiest of grins. "I gotta say, I already knew you were the real deal, but boy do you work fast."

"Believe you me, I'm as surprised as you are. I guess Fate decided you've waited long enough to meet your soulmate."

Brad broke into a deep chuckle. "Auntie Fate's sure got a funny way of surprising you when you least expect it."

"Yes, she does," Chloe said with a grin.

TWO

Six months later, Chloe sat in the middle of St. George's Cathedral, surrounded by two hundred of Brad and Lia's closest, and not-so-close, family and friends.

All of them strangers to her, for she was, unfortunately, *hans solo.*

As much as Chloe loved weddings, she was loath to attend them alone. But Jenna, her best friend, roommate and go-to plus-one, had bowed out at the last minute due to a 'window emergency'—which was no small order as Jenna was director of design at Barneys New York. While Chloe did not fully understand all that was behind the emergency, from what she could gather from Jenna's frantic, early morning voicemail, it had something to do with the Polish Defamation League and the alleged, unholy usage of bratwurst and the Polish flag in a current window display.

On the way to the cathedral, Chloe had tried to convince herself there was no shame in going stag; she was there in a professional capacity, which made it less sad, right?

Besides, date-or-no-date, she would not have missed this wedding for the world. She just prayed Jenna would be able to make it to the reception in time. Going to a wedding alone was bad enough, but going to a wedding reception minus a plus-one would be unmitigated torture.

Chloe resolved that if worse came to worse, she would just pop into the reception for a few minutes to congratulate the bride and groom, drink a prerequisite cocktail, then hightail it back to the non-judgmental walls of her apartment.

An organ bellowed to life from the alcove above and the chapel filled with a classical rendition of Jewel's, *You Were Meant for Me*. Chloe watched as Brad and his grooms waltzed in from a door to the left of the pulpit. The Yankees MVP looked dashing in a crisp designer suit and his eyes sparkled with anticipation.

Once Brad settled into place next to the minister, a pair of ancient doors creaked open in the rear of the chapel and everyone turned their attention to the bridal party, who were all as tall and lithe as Lia; resplendent and ethereal in ice blue Grecian gowns.

Moments later, the organ switched to the bridal march, prompting everyone to stand. Chloe smiled when Lia appeared in the doorway, her left arm linked with her father's. She wore a vintage gown from the 1920s that was simple yet couture, with an elegant bodice embroidered with lace and pearls. Lia's black hair fell in loose curls about her shoulders and was crowned with a lace cap and understated veil – something Chloe imagined Daisy Buchanan would have worn on her wedding day.

When Chloe had first read *The Great Gatsby* in high school, she had wondered, if Daisy and Jay were real people living in the here and now, would she have seen a thread of kismet between them. Oddly enough, she wondered this about a great number of literary couples, especially the more heart-wrenching ones like Romeo and Juliet, Guinevere and Lancelot, Janie and Tea Cake. As well as historical ones like Antony and Cleopatra, Bonnie and Clyde. Too bad her gift did not extend to photographs... or, better yet, time travel.

Chloe blinked and refocused her attention on Lia and her father, who had come to a full stop at the foot of the pulpit. Lia's father kissed her on one cheek, then he turned to Brad, who had stepped forward, and shook his future son-in-law's hand.

Brad beamed at Lia as he took her hand and led her to their requisite spots before the priest.

"Family, friends and cherished guests," the priest began, his voice filling the chapel. He was indeed a master of projection. "We are gathered here today to witness and share in the blessed union of Brad Maylis and Lia Song..."

Chloe watched teary-eyed as Brad and Lia gazed lovingly at one other. A thread of kismet, looped like a figure eight, shimmered brightly around them.

She still marveled that only six months before, the lovebirds had been frequenting the same neighborhood coffee shop, none the wiser to the other's existence.... let alone that they were destined to be together.

It was moments like this, watching two soulmates pledging a lifetime of love and devotion to one another, that Chloe knew she had made the right decision when she quit her six-figure job in consulting to work full-time as a matchmaker.

She did not want to squander her gift when there were so many people in the City looking for love and in need of her help. While some people were destined to bring joy to others' lives by singing or painting or being captains of industry, Chloe knew she was predestined to bring true love into people's hearts.

And she not only took her job very seriously, she loved every waking moment of it.

The chapel thundered with applause as Brad and Lia sealed their vows with a kiss and turned to face the world as man and wife.

"Ladies and gentlemen, Mr. and Mrs. Brad Maylis," the priest pronounced.

Chloe reached in her clutch for a handkerchief, which she always had at the ready during weddings, and dabbed her mascara-free eyes. She had learned the hard way the prudence of not wearing mascara to such affairs, as there was a one hundred percent chance she would tear up at some point. And raccoon eyes did not for great photographs make.

She watched as Brad and Lia made their way

down the aisle, and was stunned into stillness when the newlyweds stopped in the middle of the chapel, turned to face her and blew her a kiss.

She had no idea they had known, let alone noticed, where she was sitting. Luckily, she had already been smiling, and that smile remained in place even in her shock. She could feel a number of eyes on her; but Chloe avoided the stares by keeping her eyes trained on Brad and Lia as they disappeared through the rear doors and into an atrium bathed in sunlight – as though Aphrodite herself was smiling down upon them.

Forty minutes later, Chloe sat in a taxi as it inched its way down a street in the Meatpacking District, flanked by the limos and towncars of other wedding guests.

Because money was no object, and because Lia had spent her twenties dancing the night away in the City's best clubs, she had elected to break with tradition and hold the reception at Pergo, Manhattan's hottest new nightclub. Pergo was a converted warehouse that spanned two stories and boasted a glass-domed ceiling through which City lights twinkled like stars.

Chloe's phone buzzed and she looked down to find a new message from Jenna:

Traffic is INSANE. But I should be there in fifteen, hopefully. I NEED A DRINK!!!

Chloe looked out the window and frowned. With traffic this bad, it could actually take anywhere from 30 minutes to an hour for Jenna to get to the club. But, on the bright side, her plus-one was on her way. Chloe just needed to figure out a way to occupy herself until her *knight-in-shining-Prada* arrived.

As the taxi advanced another foot or so, Chloe's gaze fell upon an indie bookstore in the distance. She could not tell if it was open or not. Yet, seeing how she was less than a half-mile from the club, she was willing to take the risk to find out. Thank goodness she had worn a pair of practical flats, in keeping with her motto, *comfort over couture*, which, when uttered, always elicited a side eye from Jenna, who would not be caught dead in anything less than designer.

Jenna had always been a fashionista. It was one of the few things they did not have in common when they met during Freshman Week in college and became best friends, seemingly overnight. Now, over a decade later, they were closer than sisters, without any of the sibling rivalry.

Chloe asked the cabbie to let her out at the next corner, which he did a few minutes later. The moment she shut the rear door, the cabbie gleefully took a left turn on a one-way street, getting the hell out of dodge.

Chloe made her way to the bookstore, which was situated at the other end of the block. As she did so, she noticed there was an extra pep in her step. She was quite looking forward to being surrounded by the smell of ink on pages old and new. In an age of Kindles and iPads, independent bookstores were becoming such a rarity; a death knell that depressed her. She loved the joy of discovering a book she had never heard of and of thumbing through its pages before carrying it to the checkout counter, then onward to the reading nook of her apartment. She wondered what special treasure she would find today.

Not surprisingly, as a professional matchmaker,

Chloe always gravitated to the romance aisle. Second to that was the travel memoir aisle. She was very much an armchair traveler who enjoyed reading about others' adventures abroad; perhaps to compensate for the fact that she had not been further afoot than the Caribbean for years.

As Chloe drew nigh to the bookstore's retro green awning, her phone buzzed. She pulled it from her clutch and saw there was a new message from Jenna:

Omg. I swear Kingston Lee is chilling in the limo next to me!

Chloe smiled. Kingston Lee was Hollywood's latest heartthrob with a million dollar smile and rock hard abs to boot. A few weekends before, she and Jenna had watched his latest blockbuster on-demand, and Jenna had paused the movie each and every time his shirt was off. So many times, Chloe lost count.

At one point, Chloe had to remind Jenna that she had a boyfriend named Marco who loved her very much and also did not look half bad with his shirt off.

"Chloe?"

Chloe looked up from her phone and was greeted by the sight of a tall, impeccably-dressed man with perfectly coiffed hair. He had just exited the bookstore and was carrying a shopping bag that draped under the weight of a solitary book.

The man smiled at her, one of those genuine smiles that caused the sides of his eyes to crinkle in the most endearing way.

A smile she was most familiar with.

"Alexander, hey!" she replied with a wide grin.

Alexander Turin leaned forward and greeted her with a single kiss to the cheek, as was his way having spent childhood summers with relatives on Italy's Amalfi Coast.

"So she lives," he said. Then he stepped back and his gaze took in the length of her: from her hair, which fell in loose curls about her shoulders; to her lavender gown, which boasted a sweetheart neckline and a flared skirt with a floral lace overlay; to the practical pair of gold flats on her feet.

Ever the gentleman, Alexander's eyes did not linger in one particular area, but there was no doubt he enjoyed the view.

"You look beautiful as always," he said.

"Oh, thank you," she responded, willing herself not to blush.

Alexander had always been complimentary towards her... and every other woman for that matter. He was naturally charming and debonair; a man who truly loved and appreciated the fairer sex. Like the Cary Grants and George Clooneys of the world, he had a way of making every woman feel, if only for a moment, as though she was the most beautiful woman in the world.

So charming was he, in fact, that with a wink and a smile, he could bring a blush to the cheeks of a stalwart grandmother who had survived abject poverty and the atrocities of war.

Chloe and Alexander had been work colleagues during her time at Werner + Ball. He was a few years her senior and had always been someone she could turn to for advice on dealing with crazy clients or navigating office politics. Alexander was one of the few men she had encountered in the consulting world who was not a sexist asshole – neither in his thoughts nor his actions.

"How are you?" he asked. "What has it been? Three years?"

"Just about. And I'm good. Really good."

"Are you still consulting?"

Chloe hesitated. When she worked at Werner + Ball, she had kept her gift under wraps. During her fifth year there, she had begun matchmaking in her spare time, but none of her co-workers were the wiser. And, a few years later, when she put in her notice, she only divulged that she was leaving to start her own boutique consultancy.

"Yes, I am," she replied. "And you?"

"Still at Werner. I made partner last year."

Chloe gasped. "Oh my goodness! Congratulations!"

Only a handful of people had made partner during Werner's 80-year history. But if anyone deserved it, it was Alexander.

"Thank you." His eyes shifted back to her dress. "So is this your normal bookstore attire?" he teased.

"Oh no, I'm headed to a wedding reception."

He glanced at the street. "Ah, that would explain the abnormal traffic." Then he glanced at her left hand. "And your boyfriend... the attorney... are you meeting him there? At the reception?"

Chloe frowned and shook her head. "We're no longer together."

"I'm sorry to hear that," he said as if by rote. *Did she detect a lack of sincerity in his voice?*

"So does that mean we have something in common?" he asked.

She gave him a quizzical look.

"We're both single, at the same time?"

Chloe could not help but smile. The entire time they had known each other at Werner, at least one or both of them had been in a relationship, which had always put Chloe at ease when it came to their office friendship.

"What are the chances?" she replied. "And you? What brings you to this part of town?"

"Today's my dad's birthday and I'm meeting my parents for dinner in SoHo." He lifted the bag. "My dad's a big fan of Paxton Morrow..."

"The evening news guy?"

Alexander nodded. "The store just came into a few autographed copies of his last book."

"That's so thoughtful."

"I'm glad you think so," he said, smiling at her once more – the kind of smile that made a woman think of love and marriage and sex and ecstasy all at the same time.

But Chloe liked to think she was immune to Alexander's natural charm. *Mostly immune.*

"I wish I'd known about this reception beforehand. I would have Bogarted my way into being your plus-one."

"I have a friend meeting me. She's stuck in traffic at the moment."

Chloe could have sworn there was a shift in his gaze upon hearing the word 'she.'

"You know, I tried calling you not long after you left the firm, but your number had been changed," he said.

"Oh, I'm so sorry about that. I kept getting too many telemarketing calls on the old one," she replied.

But that was only partly true. The main reason she had changed her number was to keep her ex from calling her.

"Is your new number top secret, or are you allowed to share it with an old colleague?" he asked, light-heartedly.

"Well, it is top secret. But I think I can make an exception just this once," she replied.

He pulled out his phone, unlocked it and handed

it to her. As she entered her number, a chorus of car horns filled the air.

Out the corner of her eye, Chloe spotted Jenna crossing the street, weaving her way through the limos and towncars. Chloe's shoulders instinctively stiffened. Not because she was not happy to see her *knight-in-shining-Prada*, but because of the way Jenna's brow shot up the moment she realized Chloe was talking to Alexander – a.k.a., the man Jenna had long ago dubbed, *Mr. Sexy Co-worker.*

Ever since Chloe had introduced Jenna to Alexander during an annual Werner + Ball holiday gala, Jenna had been convinced Alexander had a thing for Chloe.

Obsessively convinced.

"Alexander and I are just friends, Jenna. *Just* friends." Chloe had had to insist on more than one occasion."

"Having witnessed the way he looks at you, I beg to differ." Jenna had retorted on one such occasion.

"I think you need to see the way he looks at his *girlfriend.*"

"Believe you me, he would drop his girlfriend in a hot second if you were single."

"First of all, wrong, seeing how I was single when

we first met. And second of all, his girlfriend is like Mother Theresa with the body of a model."

Which was true. Cateriña, his girlfriend at the time, was a former runway model who had founded a nonprofit that built and maintained orphanages and schools in Cambodia.

Now, in the present, Chloe definitely was not looking forward to a week or, worse, a month's worth of Jenna humming the *K-I-S-S-I-N-G* song. And lord forbid her roommate discovered Alexander was presently single. Chloe would have to keep the conversation between them short and sweet.

"Oh my god," Jenna exclaimed between breaths upon approach. "This better be one hell of a party because getting here was a nightmare."

Jenna looked fashionably fabulous as always. She was wearing a fresh-off-the-runway, teal Lascada dress that complemented her complexion beautifully. Her hair was pinned into a wispy chignon to showcase a pair of gold drop earrings she had bought the day before.

Jenna turned her full attention to Alexander.

"Hi Alexander, long time no see," she said with a special glint in her eyes.

"It's good to see you again, Jenna."

Alexander had a knack for remembering people's names, from waiters to CEOs. Most women would have swooned that a man with his looks had remembered their name after three years; but Jenna, whose heart was already claimed by another, was not only fully immune to his charms, she was also on a mission.

"So..." Jenny began with a mischievous lilt to her voice. "Did Chloe invite you to the wedding reception thinking I would be a no-show?"

"We just ran into each other," Chloe said quickly. "Alexander was buying a book for his dad's birthday, which is today."

"Well happy birthday, Papa Turin."

"I'll be sure to tell him you said that," he said with a grin.

Jenna glanced at Chloe's right hand, which still held Alexander's phone.

"But I'm sure Chloe can fit in another plus-one, can't you Chlo?"

Chloe made a mental note to strangle Jenna later that night.

"Alexander's meeting his parents for dinner."

"Oh. Is it just the three of you for dinner...?" Jenna asked.

He nodded.

Chloe knew exactly where Jenna was going with this line of questioning and attempted to cut her off at the pass:

"We should get going before..."

"So no girlfriend to round out the place settings?" Jenna continued, completely ignoring her.

It was official, Chloe was definitely going to strangle her roommate and bury her in an unmarked grave.

"No, no girlfriend at the moment," Alexander replied.

"I gotta say, it's one hell of a coinkidink..." Jenna continued. "The two of you running into each other here of all places... after all this time."

Alexander looked at Chloe and smiled. "It is serendipitous. We were just discussing that, as a matter of fact."

"Were you now?" Jenna said.

"And Chloe was just about to offer to take me to lunch to make up for the fact that she changed her phone number and never cared enough to send an old, easily forgotten friend the new one," Alexander said.

"That is just unacceptable," Jenna said. "I'm surprised you even want to break bread with her after the way she just tossed you aside."

Alexander frowned. "I'd hate to think she was only friends with me so she could climb the corporate ladder."

"Well, it only seems fair that Chloe would atone for her sins by plying you with food and wine," Jenna replied, not missing a beat.

She grabbed Alexander's phone from Chloe's hand, then looked down at the screen. "Let me just add a four and a zero…"

Chloe stood there, feeling very much like a third wheel in a conversation that was completely about her. She tried to see what Jenna was typing in Alexander's phone, since it certainly did not take that long to add the two remaining digits of her phone number, but Jenna shifted her back just so to block Chloe's view.

"Here you go…" Jenna said, handing the phone back to its rightful owner.

"Thank you," Alexander replied. He glanced down at the screen and smiled. "You're very kind."

"I'm a giver."

"Well it was great seeing both of you again," he said, his gaze shifting back to Chloe. "Have fun at the reception."

"You'll have to come with us to the next one," Jenna said.

"I'm game. Just let me know," he said. Then he stepped forward and gave a hug first to Jenna, then to Chloe.

"Have a lovely time with your parents," Chloe said in farewell.

"I will," he said, giving her a parting kiss to the cheek. Then he drew back, his eyes connecting with hers. "See you soon."

Chloe nodded in response even as a pit settled in her stomach.

She really hoped Jenna had not been right all along about Alexander having feelings for her. She really hoped he was just being playful; playing off of Jenna as they both gleaned enjoyment from watching her squirm. The way friends were wont to do. Friends. *Just friends.*

As Alexander walked away from them, Chloe focused her entire being on avoiding Jenna's gaze.

"Shall we?" Chloe said, turning in the direction of the club.

"Oh, we shall!"

Jenna fell in step beside her, her stilettos a melodic staccato in tandem with Chloe's *sotto voce* flats.

"What a co-winky-dink," Jenna said sing-song as they crossed the street to the next block.

"What. A. Co-winky-dink..." she said once more, moments later. *Emphasizing. Each. Word.*

Chloe rolled her eyes. She was beginning to think going *hans solo* to the reception would not be so horrid after all.

"Running into your former coworker like that. Completely out of the blue. In a part of you town you're never in. And not just any former coworker. *Mr. Sexy Coworker.* Who has *always* had a thing for you."

"You should've seen Brad and Lia at the wedding," Chloe said. "They were so beautiful and the ceremony was really, really lovely..."

"Oh you know that's not going to work on me," Jenna retorted. "I don't know why you even try. Now back to Mr. Sexy Coworker. I see he got the digits."

"He was being polite."

Jenna gave her a look.

"Alexander and I were work friends. We were always friendly work friends, nothing more."

Jenna pursed her lips, saying nothing..

"I don't know why you have this weird fixation that there's more to it than that," Chloe continued. "But there's not."

"Now you and I both know you're not as clueless as you're pretending to be right now," Jenna responded, unable to hold her tongue any longer. "I saw the way he looked at you then, and I see the way he still looks at you now. He was *not* just being polite."

Chloe decided it was best to say nothing to further flame the embers of Jenna's Alexander theory.

"I mean seriously Chloe, have you not taken into account the adorableness of the babies you two would produce? We're talking Gerber, girl. Straight up Gerber."

A vision of a baby with Alexander's eyes, hair and lady-killer grin suddenly flashed in Chloe's mind. She willed it away, the same way she wished she could will away Jenna's tongue to the far reaches of a silent, silent universe.

They approached the entryway to Pergo Nightclub, which was shrouded in voluminous, ice blue velveteen curtains and flanked by half a dozen security guards.

Chloe handed her invitation to the greeter, a tall imposing fellow with a cherubic face, who gave them an appreciative once over before scanning the invite's hidden digital chip and lifting the velvet rope.

"Enjoy your night, ladies," he said.

"Oh we will! " Jenna replied as they disappeared through the velveteen curtains.

Inside, the party was in full swing. Chloe and Jenna paused at the top of a staircase leading down to the dance floor, which was swelling with a *Who's Who* of New York's glitterati and embellished with burlesque dancers in gilded cages and acrobats twirling between sheaths of silk.

"You could not pay me enough," Jenna said, staring at one the acrobats. Then she turned to face Chloe. "Okay, so, in the interest of our mutual enjoyment of this swanky reception, I will be dropping the topic of Alexander, a.k.a., Mr. Sexy Coworker, for the next eight hours."

Chloe giggled in spite of herself. "You're so thoughtful," she replied, her voice laden with sarcasm.

"I am," Jenna said with a humble nod.

Her eyes were then drawn to the neon lights of a fully-stocked bar in the center of the dance floor.

"Ooo! First things first," she said, reaching for Chloe's hand. "Open bar."

The next morning, Chloe awoke to the muffled sound of Jenna shrieking.

"Oh my god, Chloe! Oh my god, you won't believe this..."

Jenna burst into the room holding her cell phone. She was barefoot yet already dressed – to the nines, of course – for work.

"Chloe wake up," Jenna insisted, yanking the blanket off of her. "I've got great news. No phenomenal news."

Chloe groaned, keeping her eyes shut as she felt around for the blanket.

Jenna lifted the phone in triumph. "You've made the society pages!" she announced; or, rather, squealed.

Chloe sat up in alarm. "What?

"Your name, Chloe Daniels, is right here on Page Six."

Chloe shook her head. "It must be a different Chloe Daniels."

Jenna looked down at her phone and began to read:

"If you weren't invited, then you weren't at Pergo for the poshest wedding reception of the year. Yankees pitcher Brad Maylis tied the knot yesterday and, according to a friend of the couple, he owes it all to Chloe Daniels, reportedly the hottest matchmaker in Manhattan..."

"Oh my god," Chloe whispered, suddenly feeling very light-headed.

She knew she risked notoriety every time she worked with a high-profile client like Brad, but so far she had been able to fly under the radar and maintain her anonymity.

"You're in black and white girl," Jenna exclaimed. "Well, more like high-definition color. But still, Vikki Hot Lips has proclaimed you the hottest matchmaker in the city. You're going to have new clients lining up outside your door."

Jenna paused and stared at Chloe, who was all-frowns.

"What's wrong?" Jenna asked.

Chloe stood and started making her bed.

"I don't really want people thinking I'm some kind of dating service. Or hoping I can set them up with a rich athlete like Brad."

"Ugh, for such an optimist I can't believe you're being so pessimistic," Jenna replied.

"No, just realistic. I like my client flow the way it is. I like that it's word-of-mouth and my clients are really, truly looking for their soulmates."

Her bed made, Chloe moved to a nearby window and opened the curtains.

"Well, maybe you'll get lucky and your fifteen minutes of fame will expire fifteen minutes from now.

"Oh, I hope so," Chloe replied. "I really, really hope so."

THREE

Meanwhile, across town, Ian King lay sprawled on his bed, clad in a pair of boxer briefs, slowly waking to the sound of Salt n' Pepa. It took a few moments before he remembered that, *Push It*, was his throwback ringtone of the month.

Begrudgingly, he slid across the sheets and reached for his jeans, which he had quickly abandoned on the floor hours before. He fished his phone out of the jean's back pocket then lifted it to his ear.

"Hello," he said, huskily – a husk that had melted many a woman in the wee hours of the morn.

Unfortunately, the person on the other end was happily married and mostly immune to his charms.

"Good morning, Ian," came the soft yet commanding voice of Sheryl, his co-worker and one of his favorite of persons.

"Sheryl. My sweet, sweet Sheryl. Yours is a voice I could wake up to every morning," he replied.

Ian had made it his mission to bring a smile or, on the rarest of occasions, a blush to Sheryl's face at least once a week. Which was no small order, because she was as no-nonsense as one could get.

"Gunderson's looking for you," she said, matter o' factly.

Ian groaned. "Now your voice is like a cold, cold shower on a winter's day."

He sat up on the edge of the bed and ruffled his hair. "What, pray tell, does Lucifer want with me today"

"I imagine he wants to see that you're actually working and not lying around the house having wet dreams... "

"Sheryl! Language!" he gasped, melodramatically.

He could imagine her smiling on the other end, seated in the *Veritas Magazine* newsroom, her desk impressively and immaculately bare except for a laptop, a reporter's notebook and, whenever she was in the thick of a story, a binder full of research.

"Just get your ass over here," she quipped.

"Yes, ma'am," he said, hanging up.

Ian reached for the jeans on the floor, shimmied into them, then waded through a sea of clothes to the en suite bathroom where he proceeded to splash water on his face, gargle mouthwash and swipe on deodorant.

Back in the bedroom, he fished a black Rolling Stones tongue T-shirt from a pile of clean clothes on a chair and put it on. Then he stuffed his feet into a pair of sneakers and grabbed a suede blazer hanging on a doorknob.

For a brief second, he looked up at a photo hanging in the center of the door. It was the headshot of a beautiful actress with vivacious eyes and a beguiling smile.

Four darts protruded from her effervescent face.

In the kitchen, Ian found his salvation in a freshly made pot of coffee. And not just any coffee; his roommate and childhood friend, Fitz's, own special blend of deliciousness that Ian had christened, *hourmet*.

Fitz would make a full pot every morning, leaving most of it for Ian's consumption. Ian worshipped the coffee, as did anyone else who tasted it. Which was why it had become his secret weapon. With Fitz's hourmet coffee, anything was possible.

Ian filled three Styrofoam cups with the dark ambrosia and topped them off with a plastic lid. He carried them into the living room where he grabbed his car keys and palm-sized reporter's notebook from a bowl near the door.

Outside, he looked both ways and crossed the street, seemingly in no hurry. He nodded his head in greeting to Patesh, who was sweeping the sidewalk outside Ian's favorite grocery store – a favorite simply because it was conveniently across the street.

Ian turned the next corner and walked a half-block before ascending the steps of a nondescript, brick building. Inside, on the third floor, he approached a door with a frosted glass window and a sign reading, VERITAS PRESS.

Behind the door lay a large room with about two

dozen desks. On the wall adjacent to the door stood a console table crowded with coffee, tea and pastries. Ian, whose brain needed a combination of caffeine and sugar to function in the morning, beelined to the table, passing Sheryl's monkish desk along the way.

Sheryl was in the zone, pecking rhythmically on the keys of her laptop as though it were a typewriter, like the one she had cut her teeth on as a cub reporter at *The New York Times*. Sheryl was a legend in the Manhattan journalism community, winner of three Pulitzers, all earned whilst raising a family of four with her husband, Eddie, who ran a community center in Brooklyn.

Ian placed a cup of hourmet on her desk. "*Pour vous, madam*," he said with flourish.

Sheryl glanced at the cup, her eyes brightened. "*Merci!*"

"Thanks again," he said, referring to her wake-up service.

"You know I'm motivated by this and this alone," she said, taking an appreciative sip.

Ian gave a knowing smile then continued on to the console table, where he grabbed a donut from the mound of pastries.

"Yo, what's up, Ian!"

He turned to see Pete, *Veritas's* digital producer, lifting a ten-pound weight in each hand. Pete was a lanky nerd from Long Island with a ridiculously expensive graduate degree from Columbia. He joined the fold a year ago as an intern and had recently graduated to full-time staff member, with marginal benefits.

Ian looked down at Pete's hands. "Nice weights."

"I know, right."

Ian glanced over Pete's shoulder just in time to see Sheryl roll her eyes.

As Pete continued on his merry way, Ian strutted over to an open office door. Using the hand that bore the *oh-so precious* donut, he knocked on the door with one knuckle.

"Good morning, el Capitan. Ian King reporting for duty."

Steve Gunderson looked up from the *Financial Times* and, upon seeing Ian, glanced at a wall clock.

But Ian beat him to the punch.

"It's 8:55... no 8:56," Ian said. "I'm four minutes early. I think that puts me in the running for employee of the month."

Gunderson scowled. After three decades of

running manic newsrooms and intrepid reporters with maniacal egos, Gunderson's scowl was as much a part of his being as his receding hairline and ruddy complexion.

"Oh, and here's a piping hot cup of hourmet coffee, your favorite."

Ian moved to place the cup on Gunderson's desk, but since it was covered from edge to edge with all manner of paper, he just handed the cup to Gunderson instead.

"Will you stop saying that? Hourmet is not a real word," Gunderson said, lifting the cup to his lips.

"It is so a real word," Ian said, taking a seat across from him. "In fact, if you want me to break out the fourth grade grammar, it's a compound word..."

He held up one hand.

"That combines homemade..."

Then the other hand.

"And gourmet..."

Then interlocked his fingers.

"Thus giving birth to hourmet."

Gunderson grumbled. "I don't care how many fake words you use in your personal life, here at *Veritas* we use real words – the kind that can be found in a dictionary."

"Just wait. Someday soon Oprah will be saying hourmet, then you'll be begging me to use it gratuitously in an article."

Gunderson shook his head before savoring another sip.

"So, I heard you were looking for me?" Ian said, taking a long-awaited bite out of the donut. "Let me guess, you wanted to tell me in-person how you wake up every morning feeling so incredibly fortunate to have me on your team. The two of us, fighting the good fight against the evils of injustice and..."

"I have a new story for you."

"Okay, but first... how'd you like the Patty Cake story?"

Ian had just finished writing an exposé on a syndicate of bakeries, spanning all five boroughs, that, behind the patina of pies and cupcakes, were a front for money laundering and prostitution. The story focused on Mitchell Franklin, the FBI agent whose undercover efforts led to the arrest and conviction of the masterminds behind the whole intricate and *delectable* operation.

"It's good," Gunderson replied.

Ian stared back at him. "Good as in..."

"Good as in it's an acceptable piece of journalism. But it isn't Ian King great."

Ian was in no mood for criticism. Not for a story he had spent months working on. But he was too tired to argue. Instead, he leaned back in his chair.

"Well, every hit can't be a home run," he said with a shrug.

"Perhaps. But you've had a string of good pieces lately and we both know that's not your M-O. The reporting's solid. And while the story is well-told, it doesn't have your usual.... sparkle."

Ian cocked a brow. Had Gunderson just used the word, *sparkle*?

Gunderson leaned forward and rested his forearms on the desk. "Let's just say I think I've got just the story to get you out of this funk."

Ian's eyes narrowed. "I'm not in a funk," he said with the petulance of a child.

"Yeah, and Kansas wasn't named after Arkansas. I haven't gotten a strong piece from you in months. Not since the breakup..."

Ian opened his mouth to retort, but this time Gunderson beat him to the punch.

"Or, as you like to call it, 'the mutual decision to go our separate ways.'"

"That's exactly what it was."

"Well you damn sure ain't acting like it. You're acting like you got dumped and…"

"What's the story?" Ian interjected.

Gunderson fished a newspaper from one of the piles on his desk and plopped it in front of Ian. It was folded to the society page, which boasted the headline: *A Match Made By Chloe*.

Ian blinked twice to ensure his eyes weren't deceiving him. "You're joking, right?"

Gunderson shook his head. "Read the lede."

Ian picked up the newspaper, scanned the first paragraph.

"Is this somehow connected to city corruption?" he asked. "Or human trafficking? Or another important social issue for which I could win another Pulitzer?"

Gunderson stared back at him, stone-faced.

"No? Then great! I was hoping we'd start doing *Cosmo*-type articles here at *Veritas*. You know, to appeal to a ditzier audience."

Gunderson folded his hands.

"I want you to write an exposé on how these so-called matchmakers are leeches who take advantage of people desperate for love."

"And let me guess, you want me to write this with *sparkle*?" Ian said drolly.

"That's precisely what I want. Now get out of my office and get to work."

Ian stood.

"Yes, my liege," he said with a mock bow.

Gunderson shook his head, ever-so-slightly amused, as Ian re-entered the belly of the newsroom.

Ian swiped another donut from the console table then made his way to his desk, which was in a state of ordered chaos – a somewhat happy and tolerable medium between Sheryl's monkish desk and the paper mountain range on Gunderson's.

He filled his bloodstream with an added dose of caffeine and sugar as he read the gossip column from top to bottom; and top to bottom once more.

Then he tossed the paper on his desk and inwardly groaned. He could not believe his editor-in-chief was guilty of reading the *New York Metro's* gossip column. And worse yet, that his newest assignment involved turning to Page Six as a source of information.

Ian knew Vikki Hot Lips. Had known her for years, in fact.

She was a force of nature, a femme fatale, a real-life Jessica Rabbit – with ruby hair, ruby nails, ruby red lips and a vivacious wardrobe that brought all the boys to the yard.

But to Ian, she was Victoria Marie Gjrnovic. A wicked smart young woman who had fled the cloistered life of small town America for the free-wheeling halls of Berkeley before journeying east to the glitz and glam of the Big Apple, brimming with the patience and ambition one needed to prosper as a big city journalist of the first order.

They had both started out as cub reporters on the *Metro's* midnight crime beat – late nights spent listening to police scanners, then racing down to the scene of a crime to gather enough facts to write and file a story by their pre-dawn deadline.

Back then, her hair had been a mass of curls in a perpetual ponytail. Her wardrobe had been an equally practical revolving door of jeans, canvas sneakers and literature-inspired t-shirts.

As their stars rose at the paper, they diverted onto different paths of investigative journalism.

Ian segued from the midnight crime beat to the daytime politics beat, then to the coveted position of special investigative reporter, working on in-depth stories of moral and political corruption at all echelons of New York society. Then a few years ago, upon rumblings that the paper would be slashing the investigative unit to appease shareholders interested more in the bottom line than the Fourth Estate, Ian jumped ship to *Veritas*, which, as a private enterprise, was delightfully exempt from the whims of Wall Street and the corruptive interests of corporate overlords.

Vikki, on the other hand, went from the crime beat to the business beat, then kicking and screaming to the art and style beat – which, surprisingly enough, she actually took a liking to after awhile, especially when she got to do exposés on the dramas, scandals and corruption to be found in the seemingly sanctimonious world of the arts.

When Penelope Peters, the paper's nationally syndicated gossip columnist, who had been covering high society in New York and LA for over 40 years, fell desperately ill, Vikki was asked to fill in as her ghostwriter.

About a year later, when Penelope succumbed to her illness, her gossip empire passed down to Vikki, who discerned that a gossip columnist was not just a writer, but a brand. Overnight, Victoria Marie

Gjrnorvic transformed into Vikki Hot Lips, a femme fatale who commanded attention in every room she entered; and an Amazon who wielded the power of the pen with the precision of a knight of the Round Table.

Ian respected that, despite the glitz and glam of Vikki's *brand*, underneath it all, she was still just as much of a dogged investigative reporter as he. Though he did not think devoting herself to the secrets and lies of pampered millionaires, pompous actors and even more pompous philanthropists was the best use of her talent, he knew that if Vikki reported something as true, then it was true.

So the question he was left with was not so much did Chloe Daniels exist, but rather, who was she and where was she...

A needle in an urban haystack overstuffed with 8 million people.

Ian grabbed his work laptop from a locked drawer and powered it up. The quickest way to get this story over with was to get it over with.

Did he want to do a story on a stupid matchmaker? Not even. Would it win him his next Pulitzer? He'd have a better chance of winning a time-traveling DeLorean. *Which would be awesome, by the way!*

But could he take a wee bit of pleasure in exposing this matchmaking chick-a-dee as a fraud? Quite possibly. Seeing how exposing fraud and corruption was his *raison d'etre.*

While he did not want to admit he was in a funk, he knew there was some truth to Gunderson's words. Maybe it would do him good to write something more tongue-in-cheek. Maybe he could have some fun with it.

But first things first, he needed to find out more about his target: where she was from; what she looked like; if Chloe Daniels was indeed her real name.

Via his laptop, Ian went to his go-to search engine and typed, "Chloe Daniels, matchmaker, New York City." He clicked the search button and was greeted with listings for fan fiction, fashion blogs and online dating profiles. He proceeded to scroll through page after page of increasingly lackluster results.

For close to an hour, Ian experimented with one combination of search terms after another, trying to find some sort of cyber footprint for the elusive Ms.

Daniels. He had not expected her to be so damnably hard to find.

His coffee had grown cold by the time he happened upon a link to a wedding site entitled, *Jaime and Bobby Get Hitched.*

Ian clicked on the link and was taken to a page with a massive photo of a man and a woman, all-smiles, both in their thirties, slightly overweight and wearing a baseball cap: the woman, a Yankees cap; the man, a Mets cap. Beneath the photo was the filigreed caption: *Bobby & Jamie – A Coupla Cracker Jacks Get Hitched!*

That photo suddenly dissolved to an equally massive photo of the couple on their wedding day – she decked out in a voluminous wedding gown, he in a tux with a blue and orange bow tie – holding hands as they jumped over home plate in Yankee Stadium, as though it were a ceremonial broom.

Then that photo dissolved into another photo of them at their wedding reception, seated on a patio in Mets stadium watching the game, just a stone's throw from the third baseman. They wore their respective baseball caps and Bobby's right arm was wrapped around Jamie, her head resting on his shoulder.

Ian shook his head. He loved him some hockey, but he would never entertain getting married 'on ice' at Madison Square Garden or paying out the rear to hold a reception there. Call him old-fashioned...

Ian scrolled down the page to a section titled, *Our Story*, and began to read:

Jamie: Bobby and I were both at a Mets vs. Yankees game – on opposite sides of the stadium of course! The chances of us meeting in that stadium on that day, if ever, were nil had it not been for Chloe, our very own Cupid in a sports jersey (she was wearing a Yankees jersey, by the way!). When she introduced us to one another, it was true love at first sight. The only love strong enough to make me look past Bobby's bad, bad, woefully bad taste in sports teams.

Bobby: Right back at you, babe!

Ian's curiosity was piqued. If this was the same Chloe who had allegedly matched Maylis, he wondered if all of her matches were baseball-related. If baseball stadiums were her hunting ground for drunk, gullible singles.

After some quick online digging, Ian tracked down where the newlyweds lived – in a recently purchased fixer-upper in Queens. And where they worked – Bobby as a mechanic, Jamie a nurse. Since they were his only lead so far, he figured it was best to approach them for an interview in-person rather than over the phone. People were often more trusting when they could look you in the eye.

Except... he would need to call in reinforcements for this one.

Ian grabbed the newspaper, a printout and his notepad, then moseyed over to Pete's desk.

"Pete-ay!"

"What up!"

"I need your help."

Pete looked at him with a grin wider than Charlie's when he stepped into the Chocolate Factory. Pete always jumped at the opportunity to work alongside one of the seasoned reporters, Ian in particular.

"Cool. What you need?"

Ian plopped the newspaper on Pete's desk, with Vikki's column face up.

"Matchmaker, huh? Glad to see you're getting back in the game," Pete said earnestly.

Ian glared. "It's not for me, it's for a story."

"Oh. Lemme guess, you're gonna expose this chick as a fraud?"

"It's what I do best," Ian said with a wicked grin.

Pete scanned the article. "So Brad Maylis, a man who can have any woman in the world, had to resort to using a matchmaker?"

"Either that or he got solicited by this Chloe woman who saw him as an ideal target. What better way to drum up business than with a celebrity success story."

Ian handed over a printout of typed notes on Jamie and Bobby. "I may have a lead. My only lead so far. I want you to interview this couple, find out if Chloe Daniels was the matchmaker who matched them up. And if so, mine them for details. This Chloe woman is harder to nail down than Casper."

"Will do," Pete replied with an enthusiastic grin, just as the muffled sounds of Salt 'n Pepa filled the air.

Ian pulled his cell from his jeans, looked at the caller ID and shook his head as he lifted the phone to his ear.

"What'd you forget this time?"

An hour later, Ian emerged from a subway station

in Midtown, holding a long, white plastic tube and a thermos filled with hourmet. He had spent most of the train ride trying to block out the incessant giggling of two teenagers who were PDA-ing as though they were stranded on their own *Blue Lagoon*.

It was times like these that he really missed the sterile solitude of driving a car.

Ian paused at a nearby intersection and waited for the digital walking man. A black towncar caught his eye as it crossed the intersection and slowed to a stop in front of an office building with a Gothic facade. He watched as a livery driver popped out of the car and went to open the rear door.

It was small moments like these that Ian liked to let his imagination run free. He imagined an overly pampered third wife would emerge from the backseat, holding a nihilistic Shih Tzu in one arm; her other arm weighed down by a bracelet of diamonds and emeralds, gifted by her husband the moment he took up a new mistress. Secretly, she was content to have him lusting after another while she busied herself with private hot yoga sessions... hot *naked* yoga sessions... twice a week, with a guy named Chadwick.

But Ian's cynical imaginings quickly dissipated when a glorious and distinctive mane of copper-red hair emerged instead.

Vikki Hot Lips in the flesh.

He wondered what she was doing in that part of town. Then whipped out his phone and shot off a text:

Don't move.

He watched as Vikki stopped to look down at her phone then, a second later, out at the bustling street. Even at a distance, Ian could tell she was perplexed and intrigued.

Her eyes scanned the block and she spotted him just as the lights changed. She lifted a questioning brow and watched as he crossed the street towards her.

She was wearing a cobalt blue, sleeveless blouse paired with a canary yellow pencil skirt and strappy heels. Her red locks fell in a cascade of loose curls about her shoulders. And her makeup was modest save for a pop of ruby red, Jessica Rabbit lipstick.

She was intimidating and gorgeous; a literary dame you did not want to cross pens with.

"Ian King, as I live and breathed," she said as he drew nigh.

"Hello, Helena."

She rolled her eyes. She had a love-hate relationship with his nickname for her. A nickname borne after two *Metro* news interns, who had grown lovesick with Vikki from afar, exchanged fisticuffs at a bar one night. The fight had been the drunken climax of an argument over which of them had a better shot at winning her affections – even though Vikki had *no idea* either of them existed.

News of the fight hit the newsroom the next morning; and Ian had been calling her Helena (a la Helen of Troy) ever since.

"What brings you to this part of town?" he asked.

"A story. And you?"

"Dropping off something for a friend."

She glanced at the thermos in his hand. "Is that what I think it is?"

"You want some?"

Her eyes and taste buds alighted with desire. "Well, I want the secret recipe. But I'll settle for some."

Ian chuckled. "You can have all of it if you promise to courier the thermos back to me."

She held up three fingers. "Scout's honor."

He screwed the top off the thermos and handed

it over. Vikki took a sip and gave a small moan of pleasure.

Then, like the enterprising reporter he was, Ian decided to strike while the iron – and the hourmet – was hot. He glanced at the Gothic building before them.

"So are you here working on a follow up to the Maylis Matchmaker story?"

Vikki's brow lifted in surprise. "I see you've been reading my column."

Ian shook his head. "Just heard about it on the water cooler that is the New York subway."

"Hmm," she said, not entirely believing him. "Well that story has been put to bed... for now."

"For now?" he parroted, as the wheels of cause and effect began to churn in his brain. "Ah, you're predicting divorce."

"There's always that fifty-fifty chance."

"So you don't put too much credence on this matchmaker of his."

"I don't think any third party can truly guarantee two people will stay happily married forever."

"I can't believe Maylis used a matchmaker. How'd you catch wind of that in the first place?"

She cocked her head. "Why so curious, Mr. King?"

"We're journalists, you and I. We're naturally curious about everything. Including why a rich, good-looking professional athlete would need a matchmaker to get chicks."

"I guess you're going to have to read my column to find out," she said, cheekily.

Dammit. He found himself at a dead end. He could not admit he had already read the article in full. Thrice. And that he knew for a fact she had not divulged such a fact.

"Touché," he said with a smile.

He knew going in there was fat chance Vikki would ever reveal a source or the story behind a story, but it was worth a try, nonetheless. Hopefully, the one lead he did have would not turn into a dead end as well.

"Well, Mr. King, it was good seeing you. Thanks for the coffee."

"Anytime, Helena."

She gave him a look then sashayed into the lobby of the building.

Ian returned to the street corner and crossed to the next block. He made his way to a flattened construction site situated between two massive skyscrapers – a rare spot in the City where the sun could graze upon a large swath of land unobstructed.

His thoughts, however, were still on Vikki.

God she looked sexy as hell.

But she also looked more high maintenance than ever. Like a woman accustomed to having a man in her life who worshipped the very ground she walked on.

Ian had had his fill of women the City had turned into *Glamazons.*

If and when he did dive into another relationship – and that was a big if – it would be with someone who was low key and down-to-Earth. Someone who could care less about the society pages; or the latest Parisienne fashions; or keeping up with the Joneses.

He thought he had found that in his ex, Meaghan. When they met, she was an elementary school teacher. Yet, her ambitions changed during the course of their relationship, in ways he did not see coming. But he loved her and was devoted to supporting her dream of becoming a working actress. In the end, though, he ended up with a broken heart and an engagement ring on ice.

Ian crossed the threshold onto the construction site and approached a huddle of workers. In their midst stood Fitz, clean-cut and early thirties with a hint of freckles on his cheeks. He was wearing a dress shirt, tie and hardhat that screamed, *I'm the architect.*

Seeing Ian, Fitz dismissed the workers and met him halfway, eyeing the tube as though it were the Holy Grail.

"Dude, you're a lifesaver."

"You're lucky I love your coffee," Ian said, handing over the tube.

Fitz opened it and pulled out a set of blueprints.

"I can't believe I left these in the kitchen – *again.*"

"Seriously, man, this is the third time this month. Your brain's turning into a sieve."

Fitz groaned. "Yuri's driving me crazy. I was up all last night making more revisions to the blueprints. That Russian idiot can't seem to grasp that we are already under fucking construction."

Ian shook his head. "I don't know how you do it. I couldn't deal with your clients. They're all a bunch of emperors with no clothes."

Fitz smiled. "Nice metaphor."

"Your hourmet is my muse."

Fitz squinted his eyes at Ian. "You seem... energized."

"I'm working on a new story."

"Let me guess... corruption in city hall?"

Ian shook his head.

"Money laundering for an opium ring?"

Ian laughed. "Nope."

"What's so funny?"

"It's about a matchmaker."

Fitz frowned. "A matchmaker?"

"Yep. I'm investigating this woman who claims she can help you find your soulmate."

"Whoa, that sounds like some real, hard-hitting journalism."

Ian chuckled. "This is what the great Ian King has been reduced to."

"What's her name?"

"Who? The matchmaker?"

Fitz nodded.

"Oh, uh... Chloe. Chloe Daniels."

"Poor Chloe," Fitz said, shaking his head. "She has no idea what's about to hit her."

FOUR

Chloe chomped at the bit as her taxi inched its way through traffic to the entrance of the City's convention center. She could see her client, Ella Pruitt, standing on the convention steps, beneath a huge banner reading: EdGE: Electronic Gaming Expo.

Ella was in her mid-thirties and, though a lawyer, she was always conservatively dressed like an adorable librarian. She was the best friend of a former client and this was their third session together.

Plum out of patience, Chloe tossed a large note to the driver and hopped out of the cab. She run-walked the length of a block, then up the stairs to Ella.

"Oh my God, Ella, I'm so sorry. I promise you I'm not always late," Chloe said.

Ella smiled sweetly. "No worries," she replied.

As Chloe took a moment to catch her breath, she noticed Ella was rocking bangs and a chin-length bob.

"Oooh! I love your hair!"

Ella fingered her hair nervously. "I thought I'd try something different," she said. "I kinda want to look my best when I meet my soulmate."

"You look terrific. The cut definitely suits you."

Ella's eyes brightened.

"So... I know you're wondering what we're doing here," Chloe said, looping an arm around one of Ella's. "I thought we'd try something different."

Chloe led Ella through the entry doors and into the cavernous foyer of the convention hall. They made their way to a registration table where they claimed their attendee badges and welcome packets. Then one of the greeters pointed them in the direction of a pair of escalators leading up to the exhibition hall.

Since Chloe was wearing a dress with lace

detailing on the bodice, she clasped the attendee badge to her belt instead.

"During our first session, you mentioned that you secretly like to play video games," Chloe said.

"Kinda shocking, huh? For an attorney?"

"Not at all. But I figured your soulmate might be someone who likes to play video games as well."

"You think so?"

"I don't know, maybe. But it's worth a shot. Plus, I figured it'd be fun."

Upstairs, the exhibit hall was bursting with inviting booths showcasing the latest in electronic gaming. As they fell in step with the throng of other e-game enthusiasts, Chloe glanced at Ella whose eyes shone with bridled excitement.

This was one of the aspects of her job Chloe loved most – spending time with people and doing the things they loved most.

Chloe opened the welcome packet to the list of exhibits. "So, what's your favorite game?" she asked.

"Believe it or not, *Mortal Kombat*."

"Really!"

Ella nodded. "I couldn't beat up my brothers in

the backyard, but I could kick their tushes in *Mortal Kombat!*"

Chloe laughed. "Uh oh, I think I'm going to see a side of you I've never seen before."

Five hours later, Chloe's prediction proved true. With a controller in hand, sweet, shy Ella had morphed into a lean, mean virtual killing machine.... and fighting machine... and dance machine.

Thus far, they had played a dizzying array of games – from boxing to car racing to a dancing game that involved lollipops and ice cream cones. They were now at the *Mortal Kombat* booth, playing a prototype of the next iteration of the game.

They were in the midst of a fantastical battle for... well, Chloe was not sure what exactly. Cosmic domination, perhaps?

She glanced at Ella, who had yet to show any signs of slowing down. Her enthusiasm was contagious and the only thing sustaining Chloe, who would have pooped out two, nay, three hours ago.

A small crowd of men had gathered around them, watching as though Ella and Chloe were in the throes of a Jell-O wrestling match. Because for these men, pretty women + like video games = HOT!

"Agh!" Chloe groaned as Ella's fighter locked her fighter in ice then proceeded to karate kick the human popsicle in half.

The men applauded and wolf-whistled.

"Sorry," Ella said turning to Chloe, grinning from ear to ear. "You're getting better, though."

From the crowd of admirers, a tall man with Labrador eyes and a boyish grin stepped forward, his eyes on Ella.

"You'd have a serious future as a game tester," he said.

Ella noticed his shirt, which boasted the number 9 in a Metallica-esque font. She gasped.

"Oh my goodness, Assassins 9. I love that game!"

The man's face brightened. "Yeah? I'm psyched to hear that. I'm on the development team."

Ella was visibly impressed.

"I'm Tim," he said, extending his hand.

"Ella," she said, shaking it. "And this is my... friend... Chloe."

"Nice to meet you both," he responded. Then he nodded at the game controller in Chloe's hand.

"Mind if I step in?"

"Not at all," Chloe replied, hoping her tone did not betray just how happy she was to give her thumbs a much-needed reprieve.

"Although, I must warn you," she said, handing him the controller, "She takes no prisoners."

"I can definitely see that," Tim said, smiling at Ella in a way that brought a rosé to her cheeks.

Chloe, however, was totally oblivious to this as she checked the time on her phone.

"Oh, crap!" she muttered.

"Is everything, okay?" Ella asked, genuinely concerned.

"Oh no, everything's fine. Except I have to take off. I'm supposed to meet a friend cross-town and I just realized I'm already running late. I hate to leave so abruptly, though."

"No worries," Ella said, giving Chloe a warm hug goodbye. "I had a blast today; thanks so much for bringing me here."

"My pleasure. And thanks to you, I think I can officially call myself a gamer girl now," Chloe replied, though her sore thumbs protested to the contrary.

She turned to Tim. "Nice meeting you. And good luck... you're gonna need it."

They waved their goodbyes and Chloe made her way back towards the main entrance.

"Chloe, wait!"

She turned to see Ella speed-walking in her wake.

"I just, um... do you think..."

There was a hesitation in Ella's voice, as though she was afraid of the potential answer to her unuttered question.

"Is Tim the one?" Chloe asked on her behalf.

Ella nodded. Then stood there, holding her breath, awaiting an answer.

Chloe glanced at Tim who was holding both controllers, like a good little puppy, waiting for his Ella to return.

Chloe shook her head. "No, unfortunately. But he's cute and he obviously likes you."

She smiled encouragingly. "He may not be Mister Right but that doesn't mean he can't be Mister Right Now."

"I can't believe you said that!" Jenna said.

"What?" Chloe asked, slightly taken aback.

They made their way through the opulent exit of Shanghai Lounge, where they had just attended an invitation-only concert with Priya, an indie neo-soul artist. Jenna had scored two last-minute seats thanks to one of her many connections in the fashion industry.

"Really, Chloe? Mr. Right Now? You sound like a Hollywood Madam."

"I do not."

Jenna cocked a brow.

"Hey, I didn't tell her to sleep with the guy. Besides, it may be weeks or months before Ella meets her soulmate. So in the meantime, it's better for her to flirt and have fun than to stay at home every night pining away."

"Hmm... if only you followed your own advice."

Chloe elected to ignore that.

They strolled down a well-lit sidewalk, lined with restaurants and boutiques. Their destination: Murrays, a bakery that made the best cheesecake in Manhattan. Chloe and Jenna always did an *eat-by* when they were in the neighborhood.

"My battery's low. Can I borrow your phone for a sec?" Jenna asked.

"Yeah, sure."

Chloe extracted her cell from her purse and handed it over. Jenna unlocked it – they knew each other's passwords, in case of emergency – and fell silent.

Chloe's mind turned to the Kismet Party she held thrice a year. She would have to start planning the next one soon. Kismet Parties were a fun get-together for her clients and their friends, with games, dancing and love-themed cocktails.

"The chances of finding your soulmate at the party are quite low," Chloe would always tell her newest clients. "But there's always a chance you could befriend someone whose social circle is degrees of separation from your soulmate."

"I knew it!" Jenna exclaimed, ripping Chloe from her reverie.

"What?"

Jenna tapped on the phone.

"Hey, Chloe," came the sound of Alexander's recorded voice. "It's Alexander. It was really great seeing you the other day. I fly out to Hong Kong tomorrow, but I'd love for us to catch up when I get back… if you can pencil me in, that is," he added, playfully.

Jenna tapped on the phone once more. "I knew he would call you. And within the 48-hour rule, too. Have you called him back? You haven't, have you?"

Chloe groaned. "Here we go."

"Hey, I promised you a night's reprieve during the wedding reception only. So… you plan on calling him back?"

"It would be rude not to."

"Okay, dialing now…"

"What!" With ninja-like precision, Chloe snatched the phone out of Jenna's hand. She glanced down at the screen and was relieved to see a call had not been initiated yet.

"Jenna, I swear to god!"

Jenna groaned. "Oh come on, Chlo, why are you being so weird? You haven't been on a date in *for-e-ver* and Alexander is an Adonis wrapped in sexy, wrapped in bacon…"

Jenna loved bacon.

"And he definitely has the hots for you."

"No, he doesn't. And even if he did, which he doesn't, he isn't my type."

Jenna's eyes narrowed. "First of all, Alexander

Turin is every woman's type. Second of all, you've been single so long, you're not allowed to have a type."

Frustrated, Jenna stopped dead in her tracks. "Okay, that's it, I'm invoking the Bubble."

And by Bubble, she meant the Bubble of Honesty, a tradition dating back to their college days. When the Bubble was invoked, the other person had to be totally and completely honest. No vagueness or hemming-n-hawing allowed.

"I thought we retired the Bubble," Chloe replied.

"No, it is still in full effect. So I've invoked the Bubble, and here's my question: Why are you so resistant to the idea that Alexander has feelings for you that go beyond friendship?"

"I don't think Alexander…"

"Bubble."

"I honestly don't think he likes me. I think he has a fondness for me, that's all, like a big brother or something."

"Bubble," Jenna repeated, her eyes in full *Don't Bullshit Me* mode.

"Okay, maybe he does like me in that way. I don't know for certain."

"So why are you so unwilling to find out?"

"Because..." Chloe hesitated. She and Jenna were closer than sisters; they shared everything with one other. So why was she so hesitant?

Maybe because she was not ready to admit the truth even to herself.

"Honestly?" she sighed, "Alexander's the kind of man a woman could fall hard for. As long as we were dating other people and we were just work friends, I was fine. But the prospect of it ever being more than that..."

She shook her head, her face sullen.

"I can't risk falling in love again with someone who may not be my soulmate. My heart can't handle it."

"So your Mr. Right Now advice applies to everyone but you?"

"Pretty much," Chloe replied, none too proud of her hypocrisy.

"Oh sweetie." Jenna wrapped her in a bear hug. "I get it, I do. It sucks that you can be so certain about other people's soulmates, but not your own."

Jenna took a step back and looked her square in the eyes.

"But you have the biggest heart of anyone I know. And it's stronger than you give it credit for. I know ending things with Greg was hard, but that doesn't diminish the good times you had together, does it?"

Chloe considered that for a moment, then slowly shook her head.

"I don't think it was a coincidence you ran into Alexander after all this time, on a random street in a part of town neither of you are ever in. Plus the fact that you're both single at the same time for the first time in like... *ever*. I really think you should give him a chance. Whether he turns out to be Mr. Right or Mr. Right Now, you deserve a little romance in your life this year."

"You know I love you, right," Chloe said with a teary-eyed smile.

"I know."

Jenna looped a congenial arm around Chloe's and they continued onward to cheesecake heaven.

"You know, it's almost been a year since you blackmailed me into going on my *last blind date*.

Chloe chuckled. "I didn't blackmail you. I just made you an offer you couldn't refuse."

The offer? That she would do Jenna's laundry for a month if her roommate consented to a blind date with a man she had accidentally bumped shoulders with one night, while they were en route to a spoken word play in Chelsea. Jenna had barely noticed him, but Chloe had seen the thread of kismet instantly.

"Only you would refuse to meet your soulmate because he wore overalls," Chloe said, remembering just how adamant Jenna had been that there was *no way in hell* her soulmate would be caught dead in overalls.

Jenna threw her head back in embarrassment. "God, I was such an irrational drama queen, wasn't I? I know you always say soulmates can come in unexpected packages, but it takes on a whole new meaning when it happens to you."

"Whatever happened to those overalls?"

"Ugh, Marco refuses to get rid of them. And he has like ten pairs, in varying degrees of ghastly. Every time I see them, I want to set fire to them so badly. So, so badly."

Chloe laughed.

"But in all seriousness, thanks to you and your arm-twisting, I was able to find my happily-ever-after," Jenna said. "So best believe, I will not rest until I've returned the favor."

FIVE

Ian waltzed into the newsroom carrying a deliciously greasy box o' fried chicken and potato wedges. He beelined to Pete's desk whilst biting into a *come hither* drumstick.

"Pete-ay!"

Pete looked up from his computer monitors and frowned at the sight and smell of saturated fat.

"Hungry?" Ian asked.

Pete shook his head. "I don't eat fried foods anymore, not since I started weight-lifting."

"Boo weight-lifting," Ian replied gazing lovingly at his half-eaten drumstick. "Yay, double-battered chicken deep-fried in a vat of grease."

Pete grimaced.

"I got your text message..." Ian said, pulling up a chair and taking a seat. "So how'd it go with the newlyweds?"

"Well, I've got good news and good news."

Ian grinned. "Now we're talking."

"So Bobby wasn't home when I went by for an interview, but Jamie was. She was super nice. She makes this cherry limeade from scratch that tastes just like Cherry 7-Up but like, you know, healthier."

Ian gritted his teeth. That was one of the annoying things about working with newbie reporters; they had yet to grasp the wisdom of getting to the point.

"So, right off the bat," Pete continued, "Jamie confirmed her matchmaker's name is Chloe Daniels..."

"Yes!" Ian exclaimed, pumping a fist in the air.

"So I asked her a bunch of questions about Chloe... how they met, what's she's like, what she looks like... and that's when she showed me this, their online wedding album. She gave me full access."

Pete turned one of his computer monitors 180-degrees to face Ian. "This is Chloe Daniels."

Ian's mouth froze, mid-chew, as he stared at a photo of Jamie and Bobby, in their wedding attire, standing behind Yankees home plate with their arms around a lovely young woman with luminous hair falling in soft waves about her face, her eyes warm, her smile angelic.

"I know her..." Ian said without thinking.

"You do?"

"Well, not know her, know her. But I've seen her before," he replied, raking his brain for an answer as to when, where and how their paths had crossed.

Pete proceeded to say something or other about his interview with Jamie, but Ian was completely lost in thought.

Suddenly, he snapped his greasy fingers. "F. Scott Harrington!"

Pete cocked his head. "Who?"

"An old frat brother of mine. He got married last year and she was at the reception."

He knew this for a fact because he had definitely noticed her that day; more than once.

Though he was at the wedding with his then-girlfriend, Meaghan – the woman he loved and planned to spend the rest of his life with – his gaze had been repeatedly drawn to the lady in the canary yellow sundress, whose smile was as bright and energetic as the flared and flirty hem of her dress, which bobbed and swayed with her every laugh, her every step.

His curiosity had been piqued. Yet, he was a man in love and planning to propose. Men like that did not leave their girlfriend's side to talk to another pretty woman at length... not if they did not want to sleep next to a cold shoulder for days or weeks on end.

"This F. Scott guy, you think she was his matchmaker, too?" Pete asked.

Ian nodded. "Yeah. I remember Harrington gave this special toast, thanking her for bringing true love into his life. He called her his very own Cupid in knock-off clothing."

"O-kay."

"He's a fashion designer. And a bit of a penny pincher. I can't believe he got bamboozled into paying for a matchmaker. When he made that toast, I thought she was just a mutual friend who set them up, not a charlatan for hire."

Now, knowing what the lady in the canary yellow sundress did for a living, Ian surmised he had been drawn to her simply because that was her *modus operandi* — to project an air of mystery and romanticism that caused people to gravitate to her, like a moth to a flame. If he had not been there with Meaghan, there was a good chance he and his wallet would have fallen into her orbit by evening's end.

"But wait, there's more!" Pete said, channeling a late nite TV commercial and commanding Ian's attention once more. "Luckily, Jamie still has Chloe's numbers stored in her phone. Turns out one of them is a business landline based in a home office so..."

Ian's eyes twinkled with anticipation. "You've got an address?"

Pete smiled with the smugness of the Cheshire cat. "I've got an address."

"Hot damn, Pete! Nice work."

"So what's next?"

"Well, first, I'm taking you to Finnegan's for a much deserved drink. Then, I'm going to do something I haven't done in a long time..."

"What's that?"

A sly grin spread across Ian's lips. "I'm going undercover."

Two weeks later, Ian sat by the window of a juice bar tucked in the corner of a yuppie gym. In his ear was a Bluetooth headset through which he was having a quiet conversation with... well, with no one, actually.

He was using a mobile app he had paid a techie friend of his to develop, via which an automated voice would talk whenever he stopped talking, to simulate an actual conversation. This gave him the cover he needed to sit and stare out of a window for minutes or hours on end.

He had been trailing the elusive Ms. Daniels at a safe distance for two weeks, and anticipated that she and her roommate, Jenna, would be arriving soon for their weekly yoga class.

For the most part, Chloe's life was sporadic – largely comprised of meeting with an array of clients in different parts of the city. Trailing someone like that in the Big Apple was damn near impossible. He had lost her in cabs and crowds more times than he could count. But her one constant, it seemed, was yoga Thursday with her roommate.

So Ian had deduced this was the best place and most opportune time for their paths to cross... seemingly by happenstance.

Deep in thought, he had stopped talking and the automated voice began to wax poetic about the wisdom of Cicero. "In the words of Cicero, 'love is the attempt to form a friendship inspired by beauty...'" the voice recited, just as Chloe and Jenna appeared on the opposite street corner, wielding designer yoga mats on their shoulders.

Ian sprang into action. He grabbed his smoothie from the counter just as his target began to cross the street.

"Alright, thanks man. Talk to you later," he said, ending his fake phone call.

Then he made his way to the gym's front atrium. Chloe and Jenna sailed through the front door, engaged in light-hearted banter and, just as their paths were about to cross, Ian stopped and stared at Chloe, as though she was a puzzle he suddenly needed to solve.

The puzzle of, *I know you from somewhere...*

Like clockwork, Chloe's gaze locked with his and, for a brief moment, he completely forgot what he was supposed to be doing. Instead, he was suddenly reminded that, at the wedding, it was not just her kilowatt smile that drew people into her orbit, but also the happy-go-lucky optimism that seemed to radiate from her very core.

But the knowledge that no one in New York City was ever truly that happy... or go-lucky... blinked Ian back to reality.

"Hi, I apologize for staring," he said. "I just feel like I know you from somewhere."

"Sure you do," Jenna replied in sing-song, fairly certain he had just used the laziest pick-up line in the book.

Ian snapped his fingers. "F. Scott Harrington. Were you at his wedding last year?"

Chloe's eyes brightened. "I was! Denver and Harrington, how are they doing?"

"They're good. They have a surrogate baby on the way."

"Oh my goodness! Good for them!" she replied, gracing him with that kilowatt smile of hers, as if she was genuinely thrilled by the news. But then again, of course she would be. Harrington's bundle of joy would be an added notch on her matchmaking belt; another success story she could share with prospective clients to get their name and credit card on the dotted line.

"During the reception, I asked them how they

met and they both pointed at you. You're a matchmaker, right?"

"I am."

"Are you taking on new clients, by chance?"

"Oh, I..." she said, hesitating.

"As a matter of fact, she is," Jenna interjected. Then she reached for Chloe's yoga mat. "While the two of you talk shop, I'm going to make sure we get our spot by the window."

"Thanks," Chloe said to her roommate before turning her full attention to Ian. "I'm Chloe, by the way" she said, extending her hand in greeting.

"Ian," he replied, without thinking, as they shook hands.

He mentally kicked himself. The last thing he had planned to use was his real name. In fact, two nights before, he had jotted a list of undercover names he could use and had even zeroed in on one. But all of those names flew out the window the moment her skin touched his.

"Nice to meet you, Ian. Well, you should know I'm not like any of the matchmakers you read about or see on TV. I only work with people who are ready to settle down, who are really truly looking for their soulmate."

"Oh, I'm ready," Ian said. Then, for added effect, he dropped his voice a few octaves and added a dramatic tinge of sad frustration. "I've been ready for a while."

He could feel Chloe studying him. "Why do you think you need a matchmaker?" she asked.

Why did he get the distinct feeling she was interviewing him, looking for reasons *not* to take him on as a client? That was definitely something he had not anticipated. Perhaps this was her way of adhering to the laws of supply and demand. The harder something was to come by, the more people wanted it... and the more they were willing to pay to have it.

Ian's thoughts circled back to her question: *Why do you think you need a matchmaker?*

"Honestly, I need you because I think every woman I date is The One until we break up. I figure this time around, I should get some expert guidance. Not to be melodramatic, but you're kinda my last hope."

Chloe chuckled. "I highly doubt that."

"No seriously, I haven't been able to connect with anyone since..."

He racked his brain for the just-right words to

say, an earnest lie that would get him past the velvet rope and onto her exclusive client list. He knew he needed to strike a deep, emotional chord with her. Unfortunately, the only thing that came to mind was the painful truth.

"My ex," he began, his eyes downcast, "I thought she was the one till she dumped me via email right before the holidays."

"Oh, no."

"One minute we're discussing marriage and the next, I get a Dear John email that she's fallen for someone else and they're going to shoot a film in Nepal."

"That's horrible. How long had you been together?"

"Two years."

"I'm so sorry that happened to you, Ian."

Ian blinked the pain and the heartbreak away and returned to the task at hand.

"You know, I look at Harrington and Denver, at how happy they are, and I'm like, I want that," he said, going in for the emotional kill. "I want to fall in love again, but with the right person this time. You know?"

Chloe nodded. "I do."

"So is that a yes?"

Chloe smiled. "It's a yes."

"Thank you, baby Jesus," Ian said dramatically, gazing up at the heavens.

Chloe laughed.

"So what happens next?" he asked.

She fished in her bag and pulled out a business card. "Well, first, send me an email and I'll send you an orientation packet. It includes an in-depth questionnaire so I can get to know you better."

"Okay," he replied, taking her business card and tucking it into his wallet.

"What do you, Ian?"

"For a living?"

She nodded.

"Oh, um... I'm a..."

This was something he had not – but definitely should have – figured out ahead of time. Gunderson was right; he was off his game.

Damn Meaghan and her Dear John email.

He knew he did not have the luxury of time to come up with a just-right occupation on the fly, otherwise he would look suspicious. Instead, he had to settle for the first and only word that came to mind.

"I'm an architect," he replied.

Chloe's eyes alighted with interest. "Really? What kind?"

"Commercial."

"How cool! Okay, so, after you complete the questionnaire, we can schedule a time next week or the next for me to shadow you at work."

Shit.

"At work? How come?"

"Because in some cases, a person crosses paths with their soulmate every day not knowing it. It could be a friend of a friend, or a neighbor, co-worker, or a stranger who stands next to you every day on the subway..."

"Wait, so... you're saying that you're able to tell whether a neighbor or co-worker of mine is my soulmate?"

"In a sense, yes," she replied.

On reflex, Ian's eyes flooded with skepticism. So this was her shtick. A shtick that had fooled Brad Maylis, Jamie and Bobby, Denver and Harrington and dozens of others. She did not market herself as being just a matchmaker. Oh no, she was some sort of magical, hyper-evolved being who could pluck your soulmate from the masses, like a pebble floating in the great blue sea.

"Have you ever been wrong?" he asked.

Chloe smiled serenely. "No. I have not."

There it was again, that magnetic optimism of hers. Boy was she good. He was beginning to empathize with all those who had fallen under her spell.

"Okay, um, I'll check my calendar and send you a few dates that work."

"Perfect. I look forward to working with you, Ian."

"And I, you," he replied, feigning the hope-laden smile of someone who was *truly* looking forward to finding their soulmate.

Ian continued on to the front doors and once he was safely outside, he yanked out his cell and speed dialed Fitz.

"Hey, listen, I need a favor... a *huge* favor."

Chloe weaved her way through a maze of yoga mats over to where Jenna had set up theirs. Jenna sat cross-legged on her mat, typing up a work email on her phone.

"So..." she said, glancing up at Chloe. "Did you take him on as a client?"

Chloe kneeled on her mat. "I did."

"Well that's too bad. 'Cus he's hot. What's his name?

"Ian."

"And what does he do?"

"He's an architect."

"Really? That means he's smart *and* good with his hands. Yep, he definitely would've been a solid contender for Mr. Right Now."

Chloe shook her head. "Just the other day you were going on and on about Alexander."

"Hey, I'm still Team Alexander. But he's out of town right now. Plus, who says you have to limit yourself to just one Mr. Right Now."

"You're unbelievable."

"This sexy architect guy remembers you from a wedding that happened like a year ago. Which means you definitely left an impression on him."

"Yes, a *professional* impression."

"Yeah, no. That's not how the male brain works."

Chloe chuckled. "Ah, so now you're an expert on how men think?"

"Yep," Jenna replied with a twinkle in her eye. "My PhD in men's studies is in the mail as we speak."

"That's awesome, I can't wait to see it!" Chloe said, cheekily.

Jenna bent forward, stretching her torso over her legs as she wrapped both hands around the soles of her feet.

"Well, unfortunately, there's no turning back now, you've already taken him on as a client."

"Yes," Chloe said with a smile. "And I'm very much looking forward to helping him find his Mrs. Right!"

SIX

Ian leaned on the slate-tiled exterior of a stone and tile showroom in Harlem, holding a to-go cup of hourmet in each hand. He was dapperly dressed in a pair of grey gabardine trousers, a crisp white button-up and a pair of black, cap toe shoes that had not seen the light of day since F. Scott Harrington's wedding.

It had been a little over a week since he had seen Chloe and this was their first session together. Days before, he had completed her client questionnaire, which contained an assortment of questions from where he grew up and went to college; to what he liked to do on weekends and days off. Curiously enough, there were no questions pertaining to what he was looking for in a woman or if he had a *Type*.

He supposed it had something to do with Chloe's snake oil claim that she could somehow *sense* when two people were soulmates. Yet, in the real world of chemistry and physics, he wondered how she planned to pull off choosing *the perfect woman* for him, without some sort of North Star as to his preferences and expectations when it came to the fairer sex.

He was very much looking forward to seeing her parlour tricks in action.

As he awaited her arrival, he ran through his game plan for the day. Over the weekend, he and Fitz had sat at their favorite pub strategizing how he could pull off pretending to be an architect for six to eight hours straight. After three rounds of beers and appetizers, they settled on starting the day at this stone and tile showroom, where Ian could pretend he was evaluating tile options for the atrium of a residential building 'his firm' was remodeling from head to toe.

Next, Ian would take Chloe over to Fitz's priority construction site, where 'they' were building a 5-star hotel and entertainment complex financed by Yuri

Petrovich, a Russian oligarch and luxury hotel magnate. The two of them would sit in the office trailer on-site, where Ian would pretend to crunch numbers and update project timelines on a computer. Then Fitz would show up and regale Chloe with true tales from his life as an enterprising architect as they dined at a steakhouse nearby – presuming she was not a vegetarian.

In the afternoon, the three of them would journey to a pitch meeting at a landscape architecture firm Fitz was considering bringing on as a subcontractor on the Petrovich project. Then Ian would bid Chloe *adieu* and he and Fitz would pop into their favorite pub – a favorite because it was down the street from their apartment – where he could unwind from the day's subterfuge.

A taxi slowed to a stop in front of him and Chloe hopped out, wearing a billowy dress and looking as lovely and refreshing as a summer breeze.

"Hi. Sorry to keep you waiting," she said with a guilt-laden smile.

"Good morning," he replied. "Coffee?"

"Wow, yes. Thanks. What kind is it?"

"It's a special blend Fitz, my roommate... and business partner, created."

She took a sip, then her eyes widened with delight. "This is phenomenal."

"I know, right?" he replied with a grin. His secret weapon never failed to deliver.

"So Fitz, is he an architect as well?"

Ian nodded. "In fact, he's the talented one. Which is why he's client-facing while I'm more behind-the-scenes, handling the numbers, contracts, suppliers and all that."

They stepped into the showroom and for the next forty minutes or so, Ian tried his damnedest to act and sound like he knew the beneficial differences between travertine, slate, limestone and a whole host of other tile options. He was certain he made a number of amateur missteps along the way. Yet, the salesman was gracious enough not to call him out on it. Likely because he presumed Ian was in peacock mode – trying to impress the young lady he had waltzed into the shop with.

Ian breathed a quiet sigh of relief the second they exited the showroom. Then he turned to Chloe. "You cool with taking the subway?"

"Mm-hmm," she replied without hesitation.

During the two weeks he had spent tailing her from afar, Chloe had taken the subway only once.

He presumed she was just another elitist snob who only took the train when there was no other recourse.

Yet, moments later, when they stepped into a train car that was standing room only, Chloe seemed unfazed by the sights, sounds and smells of the eclectic menagerie that is the New York City subway. They maneuvered to a less crowded spot in the rear of the car and each planted a hand on the handrail above.

"So are you a native New Yorker or a transplant like half the people in this city?" Ian asked as the train began to rattle down the track.

"I'm a transplant."

"From where?"

"Maryland. Near Annapolis."

"Ah, let me guess... in high school, your parents warned you to stay away from those horny Navy Academy boys."

Chloe chuckled. "That might have come up when we had The Talk."

"So when you graduated from high school, having not been knocked up by a seaman, where'd you go?"

"Nice double entendre."

Ian smiled, loving that his wordplay had not gone unnoticed.

"I went to college in Rhode Island, then moved here."

She was being vague. Which meant she had gone to a small, liberal arts college no one had ever heard of; or she had gone to an Ivy. His money was on the latter.

"You grew up in Boston, right?" she asked.

"Yeah," he replied, recalling that that was one of the questions on her intake questionnaire.

"I really like Boston," she said. "It's a beautiful city but still down-to-Earth."

Suddenly the train jerked, causing hourmet to spring forth from Chloe's cup and onto Ian's shirt.

"Oh no, I'm so sorry!" Without thinking, Chloe took her free hand off the overhead rail and began to wipe the coffee droplets from his shirt.

The train car jerked once more, knocking Chloe off-balance. As she began to fall backwards, Ian wrapped an arm around her waist and pulled her close. Amazingly enough, no coffee was spilled in the process.

"You okay?" he asked, his eyes connecting with hers.

"Yes, thank you."

She looked away and reached up to clasp her hand back around the overhead rail. The flora of her perfume teased his nose and Ian became acutely aware of the curve of her waist, the rosé of her lips, the sweet softness of her dress.

Under different circumstances, if he was not undercover and she a charlatan, he would have found a way to keep his arm there just a while longer. Perhaps by asking another question to distract her; or by saying something witty like, *it's not every day I get to rescue a damsel in distress, but when I do, it's with one arm.*

She would have laughed and he would have had a few more seconds of bliss.

Yet, for Ian, no matter how attractive a source or a person of interest might be, the story always came first. So he withdrew his arm from her waist and his eyes from her face, and turned his attention back to the task at hand.

A half hour later, they resurfaced aboveground and crossed the street to Fitz's Midtown construction site. Ian glanced at Chloe, who was visibly in awe of the massive tract of soil that once was home to two Art Deco high-rises.

The air was filled with dust and the sounds of drilling as they made their way to a mobile trailer nestled on the far end of the site. Inside, the trailer had a couch on one end; a desk and computer on the other; filing cabinets and a drafting table in between.

"Welcome to my office," Ian said with mock pomp and circumstance.

"I like it. Very *feng shui*."

Ian smiled as he walked over to the desk. "I feel like I should apologize in advance, the next hour or so is going to be pretty boring as I have some number crunching to do, but you said you wanted to shadow me during a typical day."

"No worries, I have plenty to occupy myself in the meantime."

She sat on the couch and pulled out an iPad.

"By the way, are you vegetarian?" he asked.

She shook her head.

"There's a really good steakhouse near here. I was thinking we could go there for lunch."

"Sounds good."

Ian sat behind Fitz's desk, wiggled the computer mouse and watched as the computer monitor slowly awakened from its slumber. Then he opened up one of Fitz's budget spreadsheets, made a duplicate copy and starting inputting fake financial numbers *like a boss*.

Suddenly, the door to the trailer flew open and in stormed a large man with broad shoulders, a booming chest and an equally booming voice. Behind him was a bodyguard who was bigger and taller than he.

The man looked at Ian and scowled.

"Where is Fitz?" he demanded, in a thick Russian accent.

Ian stood up. "He had a meeting with the marble supplier. You must be Yuri."

Yuri cocked his head. "And you are?"

Ian walked over to shake Yuri's hand. "Ian. I work with Fitz."

Yuri squinted his eyes. "Fitz never mention you."

"I'm much more behind-the-scenes."

Yuri shook the rolled up blueprint he wielded in his hand. "Fitz send me this for approval. But I cannot approve what makes no sense."

He plodded over to the drafting table and

unfurled the blueprint. "Look at this. Does this look like garden courtyard to you? All I see is circles and squares. There is no depth, no color. This, I do not like."

"Okay, uh, let me call Fitz since he's the lead on this project."

Ian took out his cell and speed-dialed Fitz. Meanwhile, Yuri glanced over his shoulder, noticing Chloe for the first time.

"Hello," Yuri said with a smile.

"Hi."

He walked over and reached for her hand. "Yuri Petrovich."

"Chloe Daniels."

"A pleasure," he said kissing her hand with gentle grace. Then he nodded at Ian. "Are you with him?"

Chloe nodded, mistaking his meaning.

He frowned. "A pity."

"I couldn't reach him," Ian said, hanging up. "He must be in the subway. But I left a message for him to give you a call as soon as he's above-ground."

"I am busy man. I do not wait. Are you like Fitz?"

Ian furrowed his brow, not following.

"Are you architect like Fitz?"

Ian glanced at Chloe who was definitely listening to all that was being said. "Yes, I am, but..."

"Then you, explain this." Yuri plodded back over to the blueprint on the drafting table.

Shit!

"Oh... uh..."

"Or I hire different firm that is more competent. Simple that."

Double shit!

The last thing Ian wanted was to cause his best friend to lose his biggest commission to date. "Okay, lemme just..."

Ian hunched over the drafting table. His fingernails dug into the sides of the table as he stared at the blueprint as though it were the Rosetta Stone.

"Okay, let's see... what... we... have.... here..."

"What is wrong?" Yuri asked.

"Nothing. I'm just, uh, getting my bearings."

Yuri looked at Ian's shoulders. "You are misaligned. That is why you cannot think straight."

Yuri snapped his fingers. His bodyguard, Alexei, walked over and wrapped an arm around Ian's shoulders...

Ian's eyes bulged with alarm. "Whoa, whoa, whoa, listen, guys, there's no need for violence..."

Alexei planted the palm of his free hand on Ian's cheek and jerked it to the right. Click went the sound of vertebrae in Ian's spine.

"Ah!" Ian cried out, not so much from pain, but from the humiliation of being manhandled by a Russian giant in front of polite company.

Yuri glanced at Chloe. "Alexei's father was chiropractor."

They both watched as Alexei planted his palm on Ian's other cheek and jerked it to the left.

Suddenly, Chloe's facial expression shifted, her bottom lip dropped and her eyes locked on Yuri as a thread of kismet looped around him. She stood up, on full alert.

She opened the door to the trailer, stepped outside and watched as the thread disappeared into the cab of a mobile crane that was on the move.

"Yuri?"

"Yes."

"Are you married?"

"Divorced." He turned and graced her with a wink. "Why? Are you proposing?"

Chloe grabbed a nearby hard hat and bolted out the door.

Yuri shrugged his shoulders, then turned his attention back to Alexei, who now had his arms wrapped around Ian's torso. Alexei leaned back, lifting Ian's feet off the ground.

"Breathe," Alexei said softly.

"Listen, my thoughts are clear now. *Very clear.* If you just put me down then we can..."

Yuri leaned in close to Ian's face. "Breathe out," he said like a man accustomed to giving orders and having them followed.

"Okay, okay... breathing out."

As he breathed, Alexei jerked Ian's body twice, causing his vertebrae to click once more.

"Do the pogo stick," Yuri commanded. Alexei nodded.

Ian's eyes widened with horror. *The what!*

"This is best move for alignment," Yuri said as Alexei spun Ian around 180-degrees so his legs were in the air and his face... in Alexie's crotch.

"Ahh, what the fuck!" Ian said, jerking his head back as far away from the crotch as humanly possible.

Alexei pressed a fist into Ian's spine, then jerked

his body up and down, causing his vertebrae to go click once again.

Satisfied, Alexei flipped Ian over and set him down on the ground. Finally free, Ian scurried backwards, far away from the chiropractic giant.

"Okay... okay..." he said, trying to catch his breath. "That was, uh..."

He straightened his back and was surprised to find that he actually felt good. Really good.

"Wow," he said, touching his spine. "That actually worked."

Yuri smiled. "I always say to Alexei, he has special gift."

Ian turned his attention to the couch, which was empty; then to the door, which was ajar.

"Where'd she go?" he asked, alarmed.

He raced through the door, looked to his left then his right. In the distance, he saw Chloe waving her arms at a crane as its torso rotated to the left... towards her.

"What the hell!" he exclaimed.

He raced down the steps and skidded right into the path of a tow truck as it was backing up. Yuri yanked him back just in time.

"Thanks," Ian breathed before turning his

attention back to his matchmaker who, it seemed, had just *lost her damned mind!*

The crane stopped moving and a woman, who looked to be in her forties, opened the door to the cab and started yelling at Chloe. Ian could not hear what she was saying, but he knew the face of a pissed off woman when he saw one.

This woman was especially intimidating as she was built like a linebacker and was rocking an asymmetrical haircut straight out of Jersey. But her yelling and badassery did not faze Chloe one bit.

Ian started walking towards the crane, hoping to put an end to whatever the hell was going on before Fitz arrived. He glanced at Yuri, who had fallen in step beside him, and noticed that Yuri's eyes were trained on the woman on the crane.

Ian shifted his gaze back to Chloe just as she moved towards a steel ladder leading up to the crane's cab.

"Please tell me she isn't about to do what I think she's about to..." Ian mumbled.

Sure enough, Chloe started climbing the ladder.

"You've got to be shitting me," he grumbled with exasperation.

"Hey, what are you doing?" came the angry sound

of a man Ian instantly recognized as the site foreman. "You can't be out here without a hard hat."

Yuri, who had wisely grabbed a hat before leaving the trailer, kept on walking.

"Look," Ian said. "I'm a friend of Fitz and I..."

"I don't care who you are. Even Fitz isn't dumb enough to prance around here without a hat on."

Ian looked over at Chloe, who was still talking to the crane operator. As she reached up to shake the woman's hand, she lost her balance.

"Chloe!"

He broke into a sprint. But his fancy-schmancy shoes, not at all conducive to a construction site, slid over some loose gravel. He fell backwards and landed with a thud on the cold, hard ground.

Ian groaned as he stared up at the clear blue sky. Suddenly, Alexei's face appeared above him. "You okay?" he asked.

Ian lifted his head and was relieved to see Yuri holding Chloe in his arms.

Meanwhile, his matchmaker was grinning ear-to-ear as Yuri and the crane operator stared at each other like long lost lovers.

Back in the trailer, Ian sat on the couch, pressing an ice pack to the back of his head.

"What the hell was that?" he said, trying to keep a leash on his temper. "You can't just walk out into the middle of a construction site waving your hands like a crazy person!"

Chloe stood at the window, staring out at a row of picnic tables. The crew had broken for lunch, and Yuri and the woman, whose name was Linda, were seated at one of the tables, giggling.

"You could've gotten hurt. Or worse."

She smiled at the lovebirds. Then she glanced at Ian and, upon seeing the scowl on his lips, her face sobered.

"You're right. I'm really sorry, Ian, with how I went about it. I hope I didn't complicate things for you... with the crew or anything."

"What were you thinking?"

"It's just... when I see two people who are meant to be together..."

"Wait. You think Yuri and the crane operator are *soulmates*?"

Chloe looked out the window and grinned. "I know they are."

Ian stared at her, at a total loss for words.

Suddenly, the door flew open and Fitz raced in. "Hey, I got here as quick as I could. Where's Yuri?"

Ian nodded at the window. Fitz went to stand next to Chloe and, not at all immune to her beauty, he graced her with his best smile. "You must be Chloe. I'm Fitz."

"Ian's business partner!"

"Yes, Ian's *business partner*," Fitz said, cutting his eyes at his roommate. Then he looked out the window and frowned. "Why is Yuri talking to Linda?"

"Apparently it's a love match," Ian grumbled.

"A what?"

"Chloe here jumped in front of a moving crane just to bring those *lovebirds* together."

"I was just explaining to Ian, when I see two soulmates in the same vicinity, I get this adrenaline rush. All I can think about is bringing them together."

"Huh... so you're like an addict," Fitz replied.

Chloe furrowed her brow, not following.

"You get high off of love."

Chloe smiled. "Yeah, I guess I do."

Ian scowled at the pair of them as he re-positioned the ice pack against the angry bump on the back of his head.

SEVEN

The next morning, Ian sat silent during an editorial staff meeting at *Veritas*. He was still trying to make heads or tails of Chloe's stunt. Was she simply trying to show off in the presence of a billionaire? Or was she just a phone call away from the loony bin?

"Hey, Walter Mitty," came the sound of Gunderson's voice. "Care to snap out of it so you can give a status report and everyone can get back to work?"

Ian blinked and realized everyone was staring at him.

He leaned back in his chair and recounted the

craziness that was his first session with Chloe the Matchmaker.

"Wow," Pete breathed, when Ian wove his tale to a close. "That's some next-level acting right there."

"Either that or she's flown *w-a-y* over the cuckoo's nest," said Gunderson.

"I don't know," Ian replied. "She went to Brown so she's not lacking in the intelligence department."

"There is something of a thin line between genius and crazy," Sheryl chimed in.

"So you think it's all an act?" Gunderson asked.

"I think, it couldn't hurt to have a billionaire telling his friends he knows a great matchmaker they should use."

Gunderson nodded. "You're right. She is a smart lady, indeed. Although, I'm surprised that Russian oligarch fellow fell for it so easily."

"People are susceptible to suggestion, especially when it flatters the ego," Ian replied. "If someone told you a rich man was your soulmate, or a pretty young woman was the predestined love of your life, you'd want to believe it too, especially if you thought there was no quid pro quo involved."

"So the crane operator was young and pretty?" Pete asked.

"Young, no. Pretty...?" Ian shrugged., "Yuri seemed to think so."

"You know, it's a lucky thing you got to witness her theatrics in person," Sheryl said.

"Why's that?"

"Because now you have a killer opener for your story."

A slow smile spread across Ian's lips. "Sheryl, you are a goddess," he replied, suddenly itching to get back to his desk so he could start typing away.

"When's your next session with her," Gunderson asked.

"This weekend."

"Okay, keep us posted."

Days later, Chloe slowly awakened to the sound of her cell phone ringing. She was normally an early riser, but the night before she had gone out with a client to a Mexican wrestling match that was wondrously over-the-top and heaps of fun, but did not get her home till long past bedtime.

She was reticent to look at the caller ID, but forced herself to do so since it could be Ian, with whom she had a session scheduled that morning. They were slated to follow his Saturday morning routine, which included an invigorating swim followed by a pulsing run in Central Park. Chloe, for whom swimming was not a forte, would be abstaining from the former.

Maybe, just maybe, Ian was calling to cancel; which would be *glorious* because she really did not want to leave the sweet cocoon of her bed.

The number on the caller ID, however, was one she did not recognize. It was a local number, so perhaps Ian was calling from a house phone. Because who else would be calling her so early in the morn? Even telemarketers were not that early-birdy.

"Hello?"

"Good morning," came the sound of Alexander's voice.

It was then that Chloe realized she had not saved Alexander's number in her phone when she had texted him a few weeks back.

The day after her Bubble of Honesty talk with Jenna, Chloe had called him. When his phone went straight to voicemail, she sent a text message wishing him safe and happy travels. The next day, he texted back, *Wish you were here*, alongside a few slice-of-life photos of the bright lights and hustle n' bustle of Hong Kong.

It was a gesture harkening back to their days at Werner + Ball. She was often assigned to clients in North America while he was always off wining and dining international clients. To feed her wanderlust, he would text her photos from his trips. Candid photos of people going about their every day; of weird-looking fruits, thought-provoking architecture, et. al. And she always ate them up, every last one of them.

She had texted him a smiley face emoji as thanks and had not heard from him since.

"Good morning," she replied, pleasantly surprised.

"Wasn't sure if you were still an early bird. I didn't wake you, did I?"

She stifled a yawn. "No, I was just getting up."

Which was sort of true; her alarm was slated to go off any minute now.

"How have you been?" he asked.

"Great. And you?"

"Great, huh. Forever the optimist?"

Chloe smiled.

"I've been good," Alexander continued. "Super busy traveling back and forth between wooing a new client here in Estonia and dealing with an old, high maintenance one in Hong Kong."

For a brief moment, she was struck by the dulcet of Alexander's voice and how it was all the more suave and masculine over the phone. Or, maybe it only seemed that way because she was lying in bed with a phone to her ear, like Doris Day in *Pillow Talk.*

"You're in Estonia?" she sighed with wonderment. "You don't hear that everyday. What's it like?"

"Beautiful. It's a fascinating blend of Scandinavian and Russian culture and architecture. And they're impressively advanced when it comes to technology. I'll send you some pictures."

"Oh no, you don't have to do that..."

"Are you saying you don't like my photos anymore?" he teased.

"No, I love your photos. I just know you're really busy and..."

"Well, good, because I already took about a dozen I thought you might like. Texting... them... to... you... now."

Chloe smiled. "Thank you."

"My pleasure. So I'm back in town the latter half of next week and I wanted to see if you're free for brunch next weekend."

"Oh, um..." Chloe ran through her mental calendar. "I can do Sunday."

"Sunday it is. You still love Mediterranean food?"

"With a vengeance."

"What time should I pick you up? Ten o' clock?"

"Ten works. But I don't mind meeting you there."

"And I don't mind picking you up. You'd be doing me a favor, actually, as Bertie's long past due for an outing."

"Bertie!"

"Yep. It'll give you gals a chance to finally meet."

Bertie was the nonsensical name he had given to his cherished, 1959 BMW 507 roadster. During one of their lunches, he had shown her pictures of his 'midnight beauty' with the caramel leather interior, just days after it arrived from a collector in Austria.

"I can't wait," she replied, facetiously.

"I look forward to catching up," Alexander said. "Have a great rest of the day."

"You too."

"See you soon."

Chloe hung up and found herself at an impasse between a smile and a frown.

Contrary to Jenna's prediction that he would ask Chloe out to dinner, he had invited her to brunch instead. Brunch was the sort of thing friends did, was it not? People who were *just* friends, who *just* wanted to catch up and nothing more.

Which was exactly what she wanted them to be. Wasn't it?

Chloe stretched her arms above her head, in a sluggish salute to the sun, and breathed a deep sigh. She shook her head and dashed all conflicting thoughts of Alexander to a mental folder titled, *something to worry about another day.*

At present, she needed to focus on getting in the zone for her session with Ian.

She was also on a renewed mission to arrive early for client sessions from here on out, so Alexander's phone call had actually done her a favor. Otherwise, she definitely would have hit the snooze button four or five times before sliding out of bed... into the shower... and out the front door.

An hour later, Chloe pushed through the left side of a pair of thick, wooden doors that groaned like an old grump; and stepped into the aquamarine glow of the YMCA's Olympic swimming pool. The cavernous room was empty save for a lone figure who laced through the waters of the pool like a merman.

Chloe watched as Ian butterflied to one end of the pool, flipped under and around, then breast-stroked to the other end, where he paused to lift his head, perhaps having heard the orchestral groaning of the doors.

His eyes found hers. Then he smiled and swam towards her.

Chloe followed his lead and went to stand close to the pool.

She watched as he rose up to rest his arms on the pool's edge; and was briefly mesmerized by the water droplets on his arm as they slowly, ever so slowly, cascaded down the ripple of his biceps.

Then she watched as he lifted a pair of goggles from his eyes and stared up at her, looking incredibly zen, as though he had not a care and all the time in the world.

His eyelashes, dark and heavy with moisture,

were especially voluminous, making his soulful eyes look all the more soulful.

"Good morning," came the deep, siren sound of his voice.

First Alexander, now Ian. Why were male voices having such an intimate effect on her all of a sudden?

Snap out of it! Chloe thought, mentally pinching herself.

Maybe Jenna was right. Maybe she was long past due for a fling with a Mr. Right Now. He just could not be Ian, her client; or Alexander, her new *brunch-buddy*.

Chloe had had many a handsome client through the years. Lusting after them was something she had never done, and it was certainly not something she would start doing now.

"Good morning," she replied, casual and composed.

"Care for a swim?"

"Oh no, I'm a terrible swimmer. Great floater; terrible swimmer."

Ian chuckled. "I'll just do a few more laps, then we can head out."

"No hurry. Just do what you normally do. And if

your soulmate walks through the door, I'll let you know."

"Cool," he said with a wink before gliding the goggles back over his eyes. Then he backstroked away from her, rolled onto his belly, submerged his face underwater and resumed his laps.

Chloe ascended the risers nearby and sat in a middle row. She banished all thoughts of Ian, his bare arms and lusty water droplets, from her mind; and focused instead on queuing up an audiobook she had loaded on her phone to keep herself entertained during Ian's swim. Luckily, the book's prose was so descriptive, it kept her mind and imagination off of Ian and the pool, and squarely in the wilds of the Amazon rainforest.

About fifteen minutes later, a movement by the pool drew Chloe's attention and she looked down to find Ian hoisting himself out of the water.

With his back to her, he strutted to a bench nearby, grabbed an oversized towel and secured it about his waist. Then he took another towel, dried his face, neck and hair; and wrapped it around his broad shoulders.

As he began to turn around, Chloe averted her gaze. She looked down at her phone and was suddenly inspired to change the photo on her phone's lock screen.

Moments later, with a new lock screen featuring a double rainbow arcing o'er a majestic waterfall in Hawaii, she glanced up at the pool, which was quiet and still.

In the bottom periphery of her eyes, she spotted Ian standing at the base of the risers, staring up at her with a bemused expression on his face.

"You're done," she said, when nothing more eloquent came to mind.

He nodded. "What are you listening to?"

Chloe maintained eye contact with his eyes and his eyes alone. Not the right angles of his pecs... or the square of his jaw. Nope, just the soulmate-seeking eyes of her client.

"Oh, um... it's an audiobook about three women who spent a year sailing down the Amazon River."

Ian's eyes widened. "Really. Wow, that's brave. I'm guessing they made it out alive since one of them wrote a book about it?"

Chloe chuckled. "I'm only a few chapters in but, yeah, it's more a question of to what extent did they make it out unscathed."

"So is this recon for you? Are you planning a trip to the Amazon?"

"Someday. Maybe."

"Why maybe?"

She sighed pleasantly enough. "So much to do and only so many hours in a day."

"Well, you should definitely go. South America is beautiful."

"You've been?"

He nodded. "Some buddies and I, we went backpacking through a couple countries right after college."

"Nice," she said with a smile. "What was your favorite part?"

"Patagonia, hands down," he replied with wistful remembrance.

"Yeah? Why?"

"It's Mother Nature as kissed by the gods."

Chloe was struck by the poetry of his words. She wondered if he dabbled as a creative writer in his spare time.

"It's hard to describe," he continued. "But everywhere you turn, every landscape, every vista... you basically journey from one gasp to the next and the next."

"How long were you there?"

"In Patagonia itself, two weeks. To this day, I wish I could've stayed longer."

"Why didn't you?"

"Had other places we wanted to see before we returned to the real world of finding a job and paying down college loans."

"You think you'll ever go back?"

"Definitely. I was actually itching to go last year, but Meaghan, my ex, she wasn't much of an outdoorsy person."

Chloe nodded. The more he revealed about his ex-girlfriend, the more she understood why they were not meant to be. She was sure this Meaghan woman was a lovely person, just not right for Ian, not in the long term.

"By the way, they have bike rentals here. If you want, I can get you a bike so you can ride alongside me during my run," Ian said.

"Oh no, I'm actually looking forward to running. I ran cross-country in high school. And, until recently, I used to run the marathon every year."

"Really. Which marathon?"

"New York."

Ian's eyes alighted with surprise.

"Me too! What's your best time?"

"Three and a half. You?"

"About the same," he replied, knowing full well he had come in just under four hours. Chloe smiled as though she could see right through his subterfuge.

"Okay, so I'll go get changed, then you can show me what you've got."

"Well, I'm a little rusty, so don't hold it against me."

"I won't," he said with a smile.

EIGHT

Rusty my ass, Ian thought as the two of them jogged side-by-side round a bend in the southern heart of Central Park. Chloe was having no trouble keeping pace with him and she did not seem winded in the least. In fact, he was wondering how long he could last before she began to outpace him!

He had not expected his *magical* matchmaker, who had an Aphrodite-like penchant for dresses and skirts, to be a hardcore marathoner.

When she first walked into the pool room that morning, he was surprised to find her clad in running gear from head-to-toe. And not in a *matchy-matchy* ensemble that was more fashionable than practical. No, she was dressed like a woman ready and rearing for an early morning run.

Later, when he emerged from the YMCA locker room, clad in his own well-worn running gear, he was greeted by the delightful sight of Chloe's *petit derrière* perched high in the air as she stretched her legs in the style of the downward dog.

A part of him was disappointed she had not changed into shorts so he could steal a glance at those gorgeous legs of hers. But it was all for the best. He needed to focus not on her legs... or her derrière... but on the task at hand – squeezing as much personal information out of her as possible without arousing suspicion.

"So what did you like most about running the marathon?" he asked, starting off with an innocuous, softball question.

"The bridges," was her immediate reply.

"Any one in particular?"

Her eyes lit up. "Verrazano."

"Ah. The very first one."

She nodded. "It's incredible that we get to run across the longest bridge span in America *without* getting arrested. That never gets old to me."

"Let me guess, you're one of those people who insists on running along the edge?"

"I love looking out at the water and the boats. And the city rising in the distance," she said with a grin and a sigh, enjoying the memory of it in her mind's eye.

"And you?" she asked. "What's your favorite leg of the race?"

"This," he said, gazing upon the pastoral beauty of his favorite park in all the world. "There's no better place to end the race than right here in the Green Lady."

"The Green Lady. I've never heard that expression before."

"I just made it up."

Chloe chuckled. "Hourmet. Green Lady. Are there any other *Ian-isms* I should know about?"

"All in good time, my dear," he said with a faux British accent. "All in good time."

They jogged in silence for a moment, giving Ian a chance to collect his thoughts before he dived in for round two.

"So, have you always had the ability to sense someone's soulmate?" he asked. "Like were you in the womb kicking your mom to bring two people together?"

Chloe chuckled. "Thankfully no. Can you imagine how unsettling that would be? But, you know what, that could be a cool movie..."

She considered that for a moment.

"Well, maybe not a movie; maybe just a short film... or a series of commercials."

Her eyes glowed with merriment, as though she could see the commercial playing out in her head.

Ian smiled despite himself. "You have a vivid imagination don't you?"

"It's a gift and a curse," she said playfully.

"Okay so, if not since birth, then when? Since you could walk? Talk? Since you stopped thinking boys were icky...?"

You're not far off, Chloe thought. She became aware of her gift around the age of 12, less than a year before her parents filed for divorce. Unlike most children of divorce, she did not cry or act out or fall into depression. Because, deep down, she had a sixth sense that her parents were not meant to be, not in the long-term anyway.

Ian studied her. She seemed lost in thought. So he decided to go about the question another way.

"Do you remember the first couple you ever matched up? Were they Mr. and Mrs. Most Likely to Succeed?"

Chloe laughed.

"No. It was actually my high school track coach, Mr. Richardson, and my next door neighbor, Mrs. Lindsay."

Ian cocked a brow. "*Mrs.* Lindsay?"

"She was a widow."

"I was about to say. I didn't take you for a home wrecker."

"Oh my goodness, no. That's why I always ask if someone's single."

"So when did you start matchmaking professionally?"

"After college, I moved here and worked a couple years as a business consultant."

"Really?"

She nodded. "I was getting promotions and bonuses, the whole nine. But it wasn't fulfilling and I knew matchmaking was my calling. Plus, this city is so saturated with singles, I was spending more and more time matching people up than doing my actual job. So three years ago, I took a leap of faith, quit my job and focused on matchmaking full-time."

"And here we are," he said, his eyes connecting with hers.

She smiled in kind. "Here we are."

Later, near the northern edge of the park, they slowed to a stroll and made their way to a beverage cart where Ian purchased two bottled waters. He handed one to Chloe.

"Thank you," she replied.

They both took a few, appreciate swigs.

Over Chloe's shoulder, he noticed a couple approaching. The man was tall, lanky and carrying a wicker picnic basket. The woman was cute, petite and wearing a pink poodle skirt.

The woman gave him a shy smile as she tiptoed up to Chloe and tapped her on the shoulder.

Chloe turned and her entire face lit up. "Ella, hey! How are you?"

"I'm great. Happy Saturday."

"Happy Saturday to you, too. I love your skirt."

"Thanks, I got it at a consignment shop in Dumbo."

"Ian, this is Ella and… Tim," Chloe said.

"Nice to meet you both," Ian replied. He wondered if Ella was just a friend or one of Chloe's former clients.

Chloe cocked her head as her attention turned to Tim. She was happy to see things were going well with Ella's Mr. Right Now.

"You live in New York?" she asked.

"San Francisco, actually. I flew out yesterday so we could spend a long weekend together," Tim said, gazing down at Ella.

Hmm, Ian thought to himself. He had initially assumed Tim and Ella were another match made by Chloe – and a recent one at that, based on the saccharine, new couple vibes they were giving off. But seeing how Chloe did not know where Tim lived, that did not seem likely, which negated his gut feeling that Ella was indeed a client.

"They're having a Parisian jazz concert by the gazebo," Ella said. "We brought along some wine, cheese, fruit and breakfast pastries. You're welcome to join us if you'd like."

Ian glanced at Chloe, silently praying she would

say yes. Whether Ella was a friend or a client, spending time with her would be a great way to get more intel on his elusive matchmaker.

"Oh my goodness, that sounds like so much fun," Chloe replied. "Unfortunately, I have an appointment right after this, but thanks for the invite. I'll have to keep an eye out for the next time they have a concert like that."

Ian inwardly frowned at the missed opportunity and he wondered if Chloe's excuse was truth or fiction. But all was not lost. Ella was not a commonplace name. He was confident Pete would be able to track her down and ask a few questions about her 'friend,' Chloe Daniels. He just needed to give Pete more to go on than just a four-letter name.

"Wow, to get up early on a Saturday to listen to jazz, either you're both musicians or you really love jazz," Ian said, feigning the upbeat tone of someone who actually gave a crap.

Ella grinned. "We're definitely not musicians, I don't think..." she said, looking at Tim, who shook his head.

"Ella's a lawyer and I work in gaming," Tim said.

"Gaming as in video games? Or gaming the system?" Ian asked facetiously, in a deliberate effort to keep things light and breezy as he secretly mined for information.

Tim chuckled. "The first one."

"What company?"

"Allegiant."

"Allegiant," Ian parroted, recognizing the name. Then his brain remembered why. "You have over a billion online users worldwide?"

"That we do. You play?"

"No, but I've seen the headlines. You guys are killing it."

"Yeah, I'm lucky. It's a great place to work."

Without skipping a beat, Ian shifted his gaze to Ella, his real target.

"And what about you?" he asked. "What kind of law do you do?"

"Intellectual property. *Riveting* stuff," she said with good humor.

"Ah. Are you with Smith Allen?" he asked, naming the biggest IP player in town.

"No, Denton, Kofi & Ko."

"Nice," he replied, having extracted the information he needed.

Ella, Denton, Kofi, Ko, he recited five times in his

head, locking it in his memory bank till he had a private moment to notate it in his phone.

A polite round of goodbyes and 'have a great weekend' ensued, then Ella and Tim continued on their merry little way. Ian shifted his attention back to Chloe, who was staring after Tim and Ella with a twinkle in her eye.

"So how do you two know each other?" he asked, casually enough.

"She's a friend of a friend," she replied, vaguely enough.

Ian studied her face, which was in full poker mode. He could not tell with certainty whether she was telling the truth or dodging it.

If the latter, he wondered if it was due to some sort of honor code on her part – a la, matchmaker-client privilege.

He recalled that, in the contract he had signed to commission her services, there had been a section on privacy, detailing that she would never reveal the nature of their professional relationship unless given permission to do so.

Perhaps that was the main reason Chloe Daniels was so elusive, which was contrary to conventional business wisdom that, in this day and age, one must brand oneself a recognizable public figure to achieve ultimate success.

By being unrecognizable, she could easily shadow her clients in their day-to-day. No one would want her shadowing them at work with everyone in the office knowing that their *friend*, Chloe, was actually one of New York's hottest matchmakers.

Given this, he wondered how Chloe must have felt when Vikki outed her on Page Six to all of New York City and beyond.

"What time is your appointment after this?" he asked, glancing at his smart watch.

"Two o'clock."

"Huh, well, that leaves a good bit of time if you really wanted to check out that jazz concert."

"Oh no, we're supposed to swing by your favorite breakfast place," she replied, her mind fully in work mode.

He had kind of forgotten that the whole purpose of this rendezvous was a quixotic quest for his so-called soulmate. Chloe wanted to shadow him during his normal Saturday morning routine, which began with a swim at the YMCA and ended with a guilty pleasure breakfast at Lara's Pancake Bar.

"You hungry?" he asked.

"I'm getting there," she replied with a grin.

"Lara's is only a few blocks north of here. You up for some more cardio?"

"Let's do it!" she said, falling in step beside him as he quickened his pace to a jog then a run.

Days later, Chloe sat at her desk, in the work nook of her bedroom, planning out her schedule for the coming weeks. She was slated to join Ella at an annual charity gala hosted by Ella's firm. Yet, seeing how smitten her client was with her Mr. Right Now, Chloe surmised Ella would be putting her search for Mr. Right on hold for the time being.

She zipped off a reminder email to Ella just in case, but would not be holding her breath. There was no telling how long Ella's fling with Tim would last. A couple of weeks? Months? Longer? Yet, in the meantime, it was nice to see her so happy. Everyone deserved a summer of love every now and again.

In fact, since Saturday, Chloe had been weighing the pros of having a summer fling of her own.

Since her break up with Greg, her ex-fiancé, she had been laser focused on growing her business and catering to a growing clientele, leaving little to no time for flings or affairs of the heart.

But now, it seemed her romantic celibacy and lack of a love life was starting to interfere with her work life. She was still embarrassed by the way she had stared at Ian's *excellent* physique the other day. It was woefully unprofessional; something she had never done before and could never, ever do again.

So she resolved that she would start cordoning off time each week to accompany Jenna to parties and social events where she could flirt her way to a summer fling with a man who was as *hot* as he was non-committal. Someone she was at no risk of falling head o'er heels in love with.

She knew Jenna would be more than happy to serve as her wingwoman in this endeavor. She just needed to keep one thing secret between them in the interim.

Since college, Chloe and Jenna had shared pretty much everything with one another – the good, the bad; the highs, the lows; the funny, the *cray-cray*.

Her upcoming brunch with Alexander, however, was one thing she planned to keep to herself. She did not want to deal with, or be influenced by, Jenna hyping it up as being more than just a simple brunch between two old friends. For she knew her best friend would not view Alexander's brunch invitation as bring strictly and safely in the friendzone.

Oh no, Jenna would view it as a stepping stone to dinner followed by dancing and smooching under the moonlight... then a wedding with turtle doves and fireworks... then 2.5 kids and a second home in Maui or Tahoe.

Which was precisely why Chloe would not be breathing a word about her brunch *not-date* till long after it had passed, definitively proving that she had been right all along – Alexander's interest was purely platonic, nothing more.

Admittedly, she was nervously looking forward to catching up with him on Sunday. During her time at Werner + Ball, they would meet up for lunch once or twice a month, whenever they were both in town. They always had fun together, no matter the setting or circumstance. Alexander was a great conversationalist. During their lunches, they would talk about everything under the New York sun – from the silly to the profound.

Yet, a few years had passed since then. Their lives were different and they were no doubt different in subtle ways. They no longer had the shared experience of working at the same company. And they had never really hung out together outside of work hours or events. Would their conversation flow as freely as it once did, she wondered; or would they run out of things to talk about halfway through the meal?

Moreover, would they be another in a long and ancient line of friendships that had grown apart in more ways than one, eroded by distance and the passage of time?

NINE

"Yo, Ian," came the seemingly distant sound of Pete's voice.

Ian was at his desk, completely in the zone as he hammered out the first draft of a story on a trio of federal circuit judges who had been taking bribes from a consortium of banks that were embroiled in lawsuits for a whole host of unethical business practices.

Ian had been working on the story for months and finally had all the pieces of the puzzle in place.

The day before, he had received word from a confidential FBI source that the Bureau's cyber forensics team had just discovered the mother lode

– offshore bank accounts with digital fingerprints leading back to the consortium and all three judges.

Ian was the only reporter privy to this scoop, and he knew the story was going to *blow the fuckin' roof* off the New York judicial and financial sectors when it hit the proverbial newsstand the following week. He could not wait to count the number of heads that would be rolling in the aftermath.

But first, he needed to craft the perfect narrative, so the story would be a thrilling read from beginning to end, with all the salacious elements of a pulp fiction crime novel – mood, suspense, heroes and villains. The kind of story a reader could not put down until she had read every... juicy... word.

Suffice it to say, the great Ian King was definitely getting his groove back!

Ian finished typing a cliffhanger of a paragraph about secret meetings at a members-only hunting lodge in Montana. Then he looked up to give Pete his full attention.

Pete stared at Ian's laptop with a lopsided grin. "Man, I can't wait to read what you just wrote."

Ian's eyes twinkled. "Oh, it's good." He leaned back in his chair. "So what's up?"

"I thought you might be interested in this. A

media advisory just came through that Brad Maylis will be speaking at a press conference at the Hudson Children's Hospital tomorrow morning."

"Mmm," Ian uttered, pursing his lips. "I could definitely use a direct quote from him for the matchmaker story. Good call. Thanks for the heads up."

"Also, the woman you wanted me to recon and secretly interview, her name is Ella Pruitt. She doesn't have much of a routine beyond taking the train to work the same time every morning. So I plan to strike up a conversation with her on the train, pretending I'm relatively new to the city and looking for advice on the best way to meet people, specifically women, to date."

"Sounds good. Keep me posted."

"Oh and fun fact of the day, I did some digging online and, turns out, Ella is a gamer chick."

"Gamer chick? As in video games?"

Pete nodded. "She's crazy good. Goes by the handle, ENess29. And she's a huge fan of Assassins 9, the game her boyfriend works on."

"Elliot Ness, catchy."

"1929 was the year Ness formed The Untouchables."

"Demure attorney by day. Virtual assassin by night," Ian said with a chuckle. "This is our bread 'n butter, Pete… the fact that there's always more to a person than meets the eye."

The next day, Ian strolled into a corporate auditorium decorated with mood lighting and a half dozen rows of long, curved tabletops accented with plush leather office chairs. The tiered rows gazed down upon a sunken stage that was bare save for a podium and three leather armchairs spread evenly apart.

A handful of reporters milled about the room. Some were seated in a plush leather chair, munching on one of the pastries that were on hand to put them in a better mood. Others had elected to stand against the wall instead – which allowed for a speedier exit.

Ian's gaze fell on the opposite wall where Vikki stood wearing a white pencil skirt and a teal top with a Mandarin collar, looking as sexy and high-maintenance as ever.

She was typing away on her phone, oblivious to

the TV sports reporter nearby who desperately wanted to catch her eye… then her phone number.

Ian made his way over.

"Well, Mr. King, " Vikki said upon his approach. "If I didn't know any better I'd think you were following me."

"I could say the same to you, Helena," he replied, leaning his back against the wall. Ian was certain the sports reporter was secretly wishing he would get lost right about now.

"Poor Peggy Langdon," Vikki said.

"Who's Peggy Langdon?"

Vikki nodded at the stage. Ian followed her line of sight to a woman who had the unmistakable preppiness and peppiness of a public relations director.

"She turned white as a ghost the moment you entered the room."

Ian chuckled. "She looks perfectly zen to me."

"You see the guy she's talking to? He's the hospital's COO. I'd hazard she's alerting him to your presence. Because, if Ian King pops into a company's press conference, that means something rotten must be afoot."

Ian had not considered that he, a Pulitzer Prize-winning investigative journalist, would stand out like a rhinoceros in a china shop during an innocuous press conference about a citywide baseball tournament to raise money for children battling cancer.

"I doubt she knows who I am."

"Every PR director in New York who's worth their salt and paycheck knows exactly who you are. And they pray they'll never have the displeasure of meeting you."

"The displeasure, huh?"

"Mm-hmm," Vikki replied, quite pleased with her pun.

Ian smiled. If that were true then, on the one hand, he relished that his reputation preceded him in the halls of corporate America. On the other hand, he would have to utilize Pete as his information-gathering wingman more and more in the future.

"Excuse me, Mr. King," came the sound of a woman's voice.

Ian turned his head to find Peggy Langdon standing next to him.

"Mind if I speak with you for a moment?" she asked.

"Sure thing," he replied.

As he straightened his posture to follow Peggy Langdon *to the assistant principal's office*, he glanced over his shoulder at Vikki, who pursed her lips in the universal expression for:

Told you so.

Moments later, Ian re-entered the auditorium, having reassured the nervous Mrs. Langdon that he was simply there to ask a question of Brad Maylis. Nothing more.

The press conference was in full swing and, for the next ten minutes or so, Ian and every reporter in the room tuned out the ego-parade of one C-suite executive's boring speech after another; each more boring than the last.

Ian filled the void with thoughts of how he desperately needed to clean his room and do some damned laundry.

Then, for the first time ever, he considered that it was probably long past time he removed the darts and Meaghan's headshot from the back of his bedroom door.

Then his mind shifted to how much he had enjoyed running in the park with Chloe by his side. He had learned quite a bit about her during their time together, including the fact that she was an only child and, when her parents divorced, her dad ended up buying a house two streets over so she could spend half of each week with him and the other half at her mom's.

And, as they had dined on mouthwatering stacks of Lola's award-winning, tropical pancakes, Ian also discovered that, in the years since the divorce, Chloe had successfully matched both her parents up with their respective soulmates.

When Brad Maylis finally walked onto the stage, the cloud of boredom lifted and every reporter, photographer and cameraman came to attention.

Maylis sat in one of the armchairs and gave a heartfelt speech about why eradicating childhood cancer was a cause close to his heart. Then he opened it up for questions.

"So how was the honeymoon?" Vikki asked before anyone else had even taken a breath.

Brad chuckled. "Let's just say it was hard, very hard, for me to come back. And y'all know how much I love baseball."

The room hummed with chuckles.

"Is it true you used a matchmaker?" Ian chimed in. "And if so, how did that all come about?"

Brad shook his head. "Man, I thought for sure once I got married, I wouldn't get any more questions about my love life. But to answer your question..." he leaned forward and looked Ian square in the eye. "Yes, it's true I hired a matchmaker. All I'll say is, calling her was the best decision I've ever made in my life."

The room rumbled to life as other reporters pitched baseball questions Maylis's way.

Ian turned his head and noticed Vikki was eyeing him with bridled curiosity. He leaned close to her ear, briefly lulled by the sweet and expensive dulcet of her perfume.

"No offense to your stellar reporting skills," he whispered. "I just wanted to hear it from the horse's mouth myself."

Vikki's gaze connected with his. "Trust but verify, eh?"

A slow grin spread across his lips. "Always, Helena. Always."

Chloe slowly awoke to the warm rays of a brand new day.

It was Sunday, brunch day, and her first course of action was to peek into Jenna's bedroom to ensure she was still fast asleep.

Jenna rarely rose before noon on weekends, which was a blessing in disguise as Chloe could forego having to dodge any questions as to where she was going and with whom.

Satisfied that Jenna was fully in the throes of REM, Chloe tip-toed back to her room and started getting ready for her brunch *not-date* with Alexander. She put on a peach dress with sheer, billowy sleeves that tapered to a delicate cuff around her wrists; a pair of pearldrop earrings; and practical ballet flats.

She wore her hair down, as she normally did, and applied nothing more than a raspberry gloss to her lips.

She was in the dark as to where they would be brunching, but she knew Alexander had a penchant for eating outdoors whenever possible, so she had dressed accordingly.

He also had a penchant for arriving early; so ten minutes before ten, she made her way down to the stoop of her building, holding a purse in one hand and a shawl in the other.

Date or no date, Alexander was old-fashioned and a gentleman. She knew that, upon arrival, he would have rung the doorbell to her apartment. And the last thing she needed was Jenna waking up to the sound of door chimes. So she was pre-empting all of that by standing outside instead.

Moments later, she watched as a vintage convertible turned onto her street. The top was down and Alexander's perfectly coiffed hair flirted with the breeze as he slowed to a stop in front of her.

He glided out of the car and greeted her with that movie star smile of his. "I'm not late am I?"

"No. Jenna's asleep and I didn't want the doorbell to wake her. Plus, it's so nice out today."

Alexander was dressed dapper-casual in a blue-grey summer knit top with the sleeves rolled up mid-arm; paired with crisp, white trousers and grey-suede loafers.

"You look beautiful as always," he said, giving her a kiss to the cheek.

"And you are complimentary as always."

"I never give a compliment unless it comes

straight from the heart," he said, his eyes connecting with hers.

Most women would have swooned at that, but Chloe knew this was just Alexander's way. He had a genetic trifecta of looks, voice and charm that made even the mundane sound swoon-worthy.

"Chloe, allow me to introduce you to Bertie, the love of my life," he said, opening the passenger side door for her.

"Ah, and is it a requited love?"

"Every time I ask her how she feels about me, all she does is hum in reply."

Chloe laughed as she settled into a soft leather seat that was as cozy as a warm hug. Alexander rounded the car, glided back into the driver's seat and turned to face her.

"Top up or down?"

"Definitely down," she said, knowing full well it would wreck havoc on her hair, but not caring in the least.

"And, on a scale of one to ten, how hungry are you?" he asked.

"I had a bowl of cereal earlier, so I'd say I'm about a four right now."

Alexander shifted Bertie into gear and she purred as they pulled onto the street.

"Where are we headed?" Chloe asked.

"Greenwich."

"The Village? So, in other words, we're going to spend half an hour looking for parking."

He chuckled. "Firstly, I would never be so cruel as to park my dear, sweet, sensitive Bertie on the street."

"Oh gawd," she said with a roll of the eyes.

"Secondly, we're going to the other Greenwich."

Chloe furrowed her brow. "In *Connecticut?*"

Alexander nodded.

"That's like an hour away."

"That's the great thing about Bertie," he said with a grin as he shifted to a higher gear. "She'll get us there in half the time."

Twenty-five minutes and no speeding tickets later, Bertie rounded the circular driveway of a seaside restaurant that looked like it had teleported in from the south of France.

Alexander left Bertie in the care of a seasoned

valet and escorted Chloe into the restaurant's foyer, which was abuzz with couples, families and brunch buddies, all in wait and want of the next free table.

"Good morning, Frederick," Alexander said, having committed the maitre'd's name to memory, as was his way.

Frederick's face lit up. "Alexander, good to see you again." His eyes shifted to Chloe. "And who is this?"

"This is Chloe."

"Mademoiselle," Frederick said, taking her hand and bringing it to his lips. "It is a pleasure to meet you. Please, let me show you to your table."

They followed him though the restaurant to the semi-secluded nook of an expansive, outdoor patio with sweeping views of the marina – where alabaster yachts bobbed like gulls upon the sea.

The day was warm, with just enough breeze to keep everyone comfortable and in high spirits.

They proceeded to order that which caught their fancy on the menu, alongside a bottle of Madeira rosé.

"My mother says hi, by the way," Alexander said when the waiter left them alone with a ramekin of housemade, herbal butter and a basket of fresh croissants.

"Oh, how's Evelyn doing?" she asked, touched that his mother still remembered who she was. They had met on two occasions and Chloe had found her to be as posh as she was lovely, the product of an Upper West Side upbringing paired with years spent working in the Peace Corps and for the United Nations. Evidently, Evelyn had a gift for remembering names and faces, just like her son.

"She's good. She's currently obsessed with urban farming," he said with a prolonged sigh. "And you know how she gets when she's obsessed. Right now, I have more fruits and vegetables in my fridge than I know what to do with."

Chloe laughed. "That's rich seeing how you're always traveling."

"She has a fresh batch delivered the moment I get back in town, even if I'm only here for a few days at a time."

"She just wants you to grow up to be a *big, strong boy*," Chloe teased.

Alexander chuckled softly as he took a sip of rosé.

"So are you still loving this jet-setting lifestyle of yours?" she asked.

"Some days, yes. Other days I think to myself, why am I paying so much for an apartment I'm hardly ever in. Once I made partner, I was hoping I'd be able to command a bit more balance in my life, but so far I've been swamped putting out one international fire after another."

Chloe frowned. "I'm sorry."

"Luckily, knock on wood, I think things are starting to calm down a bit, so maybe I'll get my wish in a month or so."

"When do you fly out next?"

"Wednesday to Buenos Aires, then Berlin, then back to Hong Kong."

Chloe sighed as she gazed up at the big blue sky. "I envy you and I don't envy you."

Alexander's eyes smiled. He leaned back in his chair, fully relaxed as though he were on siesta on the shores of the Mediterranean.

"So tell me about this consultancy of yours," he said. "I'm glad to see it's going well."

"How can you tell," she asked, meeting his gaze.

"Because you're happy."

Chloe considered that for a moment, then a serene grin spread across her face. "Yeah, I am."

As his question continued to hang in the air, Chloe was at a crossroads as to how she wanted to answer.

Alexander was the colleague she had been closest to during her time at Werner + Ball. The work buddy in whom she had confided her trials and her triumphs when it came to clients, bosses and everyone in between.

But in spite of this, she had never shared her secret with him. Or with anyone at work for that matter. Taking a cue from a World War II propaganda poster that hung on the wall of her grandfather's study – 'Loose Lips Sink Ships' – she had always kept a distinct demarcation line between work and personal, to keep the latter from negatively affecting her success and reputation with the former.

For she knew everyone was as not as open-minded about gifted matchmakers as her soulmate-seeking clients were.

Back before she had decided to quit her job and devote herself to matchmaking full-time, she feared and knew in her bones that if certain colleagues, clients and higher-ups found out she was moonlighting as a matchmaker for hire, they would question her credibility; or her mental acuity; or her dedication to the job.

It was hard enough being a woman in corporate America. She thought it best not to add more fuel to the fire.

She was not sure why she had never shared her secret with Alexander. It was not due to a lack of trust on her part. Alexander was an upstanding guy; the kind of guy who would take a friend's secrets to his grave.

Yet, even during her final days at Werner, she still had not confided in him about her real reason for leaving. Saying only that she was planning to do some boutique consulting work; giving him and everyone else at the company the unspoken impression that she would be working with business clients... not people in search of true love.

She supposed she had done so out of habit. And also out of a strategic fear that if her foray into full-time entrepreneurship did not go as well as she hoped, she could return to the world of corporate consulting, her stalwart reputation still intact.

Now here she was, three years later. Business was

going quite well and, gods willing, she had no intention of returning to corporate America. Yet, inexplicably, a part of her was still reticent to share her secret with Alexander.

She decided it would be best to take baby steps; to first gauge his appetite for the abstruse.

"Do you believe in Fate?" she asked, her heart beating faster than normal.

"I do," he said without hesitation, his gaze unwavering.

Chloe blinked, she had not expected him to answer so quickly or so confidently.

"Case in point..." he continued. "Us sitting here right now. We haven't seen or talked to each other for years, then we cross paths on a random street, on a random day, under circumstances that will never repeat themselves during our lifetimes."

"You think that was Fate?"

"I do."

Given his sentiment, Chloe was surprised the topic of Fate and Destiny had never come up during one of their lunches.

"Have you always believed in Fate?" she asked. "Or is this a new POV for you?"

He mulled it over for a moment. "I think I've

come to believe in it more as I've gotten older. When I look back over my life thus far, I can see how all these little pieces and experiences have fallen perfectly into place. Order amidst the everyday chaos and uncertainty of life."

Chloe looked down at her hands and cleared her throat.

"Do you think the weavings of Fate apply to love as well? Romantic love I mean."

"Are you asking if I think Fate dictates who we fall in love with?"

"Yes."

He studied her for a moment. "What do you think?" he asked, volleying the question back to her, his curiosity piqued.

Chloe smoothed a few strands of hair behind her ear as her heart quickened its nervous pace once more.

"I believe that, in the weavings of Fate, soulmates are inextricably linked to one another and they are destined to cross paths at least once in their lifetimes, sometimes without realizing it."

"I see," he said, his face unreadable. She could not tell what he was thinking; whether he was intrigued or secretly itching to get the check.

And in that moment, Chloe realized she was much more concerned with what Alexander would think, and how he would react, than she had anticipated. She did not know why. They had been out of touch for a few years. And she had shaped an entrepreneurial life for herself that she was proud of. One in which she had the honor and pleasure of making a true and lasting difference in people's lives. She was living her purpose, she was happy. That was all that mattered.

She lifted her gaze to meet his, mentally squared her shoulders, and breathed away the nervous beating of her heart.

"My consultancy... it's a matchmaking agency. I help people find their soulmate."

"Huh," came the sound of Alexander's voice as he sat there, taking it all in.

Chloe watched as he began to slowly nod his head. "Chloe the Matchmaker," he said at long last. "I can see that."

She blinked with surprise. "Really?"

"I remember once, we all went to happy hour to celebrate Veronica's birthday and there was this guy there, Darryl from accounts payable. I remember how you sidled up to him halfway through the night and steered him to the other end of the bar where there was a group of women sipping sangria. And next thing you know, Darryl's smitten with one of the women, phone numbers were exchanged and a year later, they were man and wife.

Chloe's jaw dropped. She had no idea Alexander had been paying attention to her shenanigans that night. Was she not as subtle as she thought she had been?

Despite her creed to keep her gift secret from her co-workers, on occasions when the thread of kismet suddenly made an appearance during a business meeting, holiday party, happy hour or the like, she felt just as compelled to nudge the wandering soulmates together, if need be. To maintain her professionalism, however, she had had to figure out subtle and creative ways to do so, such as pretending to be a fun-loving wingwoman to Darryl from accounts payment, just to get him to talk to and ask out Tyra, the pretty woman he had been eyeing from afar for over an hour.

Tyra had been surrounded by four other women. It was hard enough for a shy guy like Darryl to work up the courage to approach a woman one-on-one.

There was no way he was going to approach a group of five women; not without some help.

Since Chloe and Darryl worked at the same company, she could not tell him outright: *I'm a matchmaker and I know who your soulmate is.* Instead, she had to present herself as nothing more than a temporary wingwoman; just a work colleague wanting to *help a brother out.*

But, apparently, Alexander had seen through her ruse.

"I always thought that was a nice thing you did for Darryl," Alexander said. "Did you know they have two kids now?"

"No way!"

"The youngest is named Chloe..."

Chloe gasped, bringing a hand to her heart.

"Well, it's her middle name. But still," he added.

Chloe could not believe they had named a daughter after her. Assuming they did not have a Grandma Chloe or Great-Aunt Chloe in the family, she was honored beyond words.

"And I remember that time you became laser-focused on the keynote speaker at that innovation conference we went to in Seattle..."

She frowned. "Was I that obvious?

"No, I'm just very observant."

The waiter returned with a cornucopia of mouthwatering appetizers.

"I thought it was just a fun hobby of yours," Alexander said, placing a cloth napkin in his lap. "I didn't know it was something you wanted to do full time. Is that why you left Werner?"

She nodded.

"Well, good for you," he said with a smile; and Chloe knew him well enough to know the smile was sincere.

"How many matches have you had thus far?" he asked.

"You know what," she said, blushing with embarrassment. "I don't keep count, actually."

"Then business must be *really* good."

Chloe grinned. Business had indeed been really good of late.

"You'll have to ask Jenna," she replied. "She's always keeping a tally in her head."

"Glad to see you two are still thick as thieves."

"Yeah, we are," Chloe said, trying to ignore the pit of guilt in her stomach.

She had been lying by omission to her best friend

for over a week, even going so far as to tip-toe around the house earlier, like a thief in the morn.

She promised herself she would tell Jenna everything later that week... once Alexander had jetted off to his next round of corporate fire fighting and wine-and-dines, on three continents.

Hours later, Bertie slowed to a stop in front of Chloe's apartment building.

During brunch, a subsequent stroll in the marina, and the drive back to the City, they had talked about everything under the sun, just like old times.

Chloe was beyond relieved that all of her nervousness going into the brunch had been for naught.

Alexander got out, rounded the car and opened the door for her.

"Thank you," she replied.

"It was really nice catching up," he said. "We should do this again sometime... presuming I didn't bore you to death."

Chloe smiled. "You didn't and I'd like that."

"I almost forgot..."

He popped the trunk and pulled out a sturdy canvas bag filled to the brim with a seasonal assortment of fruits and vegetables.

"For you and Jenna, courtesy of my mother... by way of my refrigerator."

Chloe laughed. "Why thank you."

He leaned in and gave her his signature kiss to the cheek. "Have a great week."

"You too. And have a safe flight... or rather, series of flights."

He grinned. "I'll send you some pics from Buenos Aires."

Then he glided back into his beloved convertible and, with a wink and a wave, jetted off into the distance.

Chloe stood there for a moment, not sure how she felt or wanted to feel as his parting words echoed in her head:

We should do this again sometime.

Sometime was vague and noncommittal.

Do this again was just as vague.

Alexander was normally very precise with his words. And she was way past the age of dissecting a cute guy's words like a moonstruck teenager.

If she took those six simple words at face value,

then he was simply saying he would like to have another friendly brunch with her at some indefinite time in the future.

Could be weeks, months, years from now.

Which meant there was a ninety-nine percent chance that, despite Jenna's incessant assertions to the contrary, Chloe had been right all along – Alexander was and always had been interested in being *just friends*.

Yet, as she stood there by the curb, his cologne still lingering in the air around her, a small hidden part of her was a wee bit disappointed by this definitive discovery.

She chalked it up to the fact that it had been a good long while since she had spent a fun and relaxing day in the company of a gorgeous man who was not a client. Male attention could be incredibly intoxicating, especially when it was showered upon you by a man like Alexander Turin.

And now that he was gone, she felt like her day was suddenly a little less sunny.

Chloe took it as a sign that having a summer fling with a Mr. Right Now who was cute, fun and in no way interested in anything long-term was *precisely* what she needed right now.

She smiled to herself as she stepped into her apartment building, excited to find out just who her Mr. Right Now would be and what kind of adventures they would get up to in the heat and vibrancy of a New York City summer.

TEN

Ian stood before his bathroom mirror, humming along to a song on the radio as he shaved his jawline.

Two weeks had passed since his session with Chloe in Central Park, and he was readying himself for their third session that night, which he was psyched about since they would be partaking of one of his guilty pleasures – something none of his hockey-loving guy friends knew about, except Fitz.

Originally, they had planned to go to a WNBA preseason game. On Chloe's client questionnaire, in reply to a question about his sports-related hobbies, Ian had falsely divulged that he *loved* to go to live WNBA games... because there was slim chance he would run into anyone he actually knew who could unwittingly blow his cover.

Earlier that week, however, Ian had gotten an email alert reminding him that he had two VIP tickets to see Celeste that Saturday. Celeste was a theatrical troupe from South Africa that was akin to Cirque du Soleil, except their show was conducted entirely in the air. They upped the ante and artistry every year and he never missed an opportunity to see them when they were in town. Which was why he always purchased VIP tickets a year in advance.

As luck would have it, his tickets were reserved for the same night as the basketball game. Even though he could have switched his session to a different night, he had a hunch Chloe would love the show as much as he did.

Now, here he was, on the cusp of going out on a Saturday night with a woman who was neither a girlfriend nor a girlfriend-to-be, with VIP tickets he had purchased a year ago with zero doubt in his mind that Meaghan would be accompanying him as his plus-one and wife-to-be.

My what a difference a few months, a Dear John email and a gossip column make, he thought.

Then for a brief, ever so brief moment, Ian allowed his mind to wander and ponder what his life would be like if Meaghan had run off with that director guy months earlier – i.e., before Harrington's wedding last summer.

What if he had been single to mingle when his gaze first fell upon the woman in the canary yellow sundress?

Undoubtedly, before nightfall, he would have introduced himself as Ian King, a journalist… not an architect. He would have regaled her with fun tales of undercover investigations past. Then they would have segued into talking, perhaps, about their mutual love of running and wanderlust for sights and cultures beyond the great blue sea.

Ian was unsure how he would have reacted when she shared *how* she did what she did for a living.

Granted, based on what he knew about Chloe thus far, namely how elusive she was outside her circle of clients and close friends, he doubted she would have shared that with him right off the bat.

Weeks later, when he had shored up her trust to the point where she felt comfortable bringing him fully into her inner circle, he would have been too far gone and *head over sneaker heels* to bother with journalistic and scientific skepticism.

And instead of spending the holiday season wallowing in a post-breakup funk of booze, darts and snarky sarcasm, he could have been spending it with her... cuddled up on his rooftop, watching New Year's Eve fireworks dancing upon the midnight sky.

Ian sighed himself out of his fanciful reverie and back into the real world where he was a reporter undercover, currently deceiving a woman who was turning out to be not at all what he and Gunderson had expected.

He still was not one-hundred percent sold on this magical, matchmaking gift of hers, but he was definitely leaning towards the conclusion that Chloe did not have a malicious or avaricious bone in her body.

He pondered that maybe he should portray her not as the villain of his story, but as the exception. A respectable matchmaker whose methods were unorthodox and required a *serious* suspension of disbelief, but who seemed to have quite the batting average of matches resulting in love and marriage and babies, galore.

Meanwhile, across town, Chloe stood before a floor-length mirror in her bedroom putting on her favorite charm bracelet.

Ian had called her earlier that week to see if, for their third session, she would be okay switching out tonight's WNBA game with something "a thousand times *awesom-er!*"

She had agreed, her curiosity piqued, especially when he provided no details beyond a recommendation to dress warm and comfortably.

Not sure how warm he was talking, she had settled upon an ankle-length maxi dress paired with a cute denim jacket and a pair of white sneakers. She also planned to bring along a Parisian scarf for added warmth if need be.

As Chloe gave herself a once-over in the mirror, the sound of door chimes filled the air.

"Can you get that?" Jenna hollered from the inner sanctum of her bedroom. "I'm on the toilet."

"T-M-I," Chloe volleyed back as she made her way to the front door.

She was fairly certain it was Jenna's boyfriend, Marco, but she checked the keyhole just in case.

Sure enough, it was Marco wearing a designer jacket Jenna had gifted on his birthday. Though her roommate was fighting a losing battle in her campaign to purge Marco's work overalls, she was steadily making upgrades to other parts of his wardrobe in the process.

Chloe opened the door and, just as she was about to give him a warm hug, the scent of Korean BBQ hot wings danced upon her nose in full *come hither* mode.

"Oh my god," she gasped, looking down at the large carry-out bags in his hand. "You brought K-Pow!"

Marco chuckled. "Yeah, and I brought enough to feed a family of six... seeing how you and Jenna run through these like industrial vacuum cleaners.

He made his way to the kitchen and Chloe followed; for he was the Pied Piper and the K-Pow his hypnotic flute.

"So, what are we watching tonight?" he asked, setting the bags on the kitchen counter.

Saturday movie night had been a monthly tradition since Chloe and Jenna moved to the City. Boyfriends were welcome to join as long as they brought yummy food and respected the fact that they had zero say in the movie lineup.

"I don't know," Chloe replied. "I have to bow out tonight."

"Hot date?"

"Session with a client."

"But she looks like she's going on a hot date, doesn't she?" Jenna said, padding into the room.

"What? No. This is a normal dress. I've worn it numerous times."

"Not like that you haven't. But hey, I get it. You're meeting up with Mr. Sexy Architect so..."

Jenna beelined past Marco, straight to the carryout bags.

"Um, boyfriend here, who you haven't seen in like a month," he said, melodramatically.

Jenna looked his way, her eyes softened. She doubled back, stood on her toes and gave him the sweetest of kisses.

"Your guilt trip won't work on me, seeing how I met you at the airport yesterday," she said, returning her full attention to the K-Pow bags.

"Oh, but it did work. I just got a kiss out of it, didn't I?" he replied with a wink.

Jenna opened one of the cartons stuffed with BBQ wings and Chloe's eyes and mind glazed over.

Jenna laughed. "Girl you might as well put on that apron over there because we both know you're not leaving here without a few of these in your belly."

Lacking any willpower whatsoever, Chloe wrapped an apron around the front of her dress. Then she dipped her hand into the carton, pulled out a delectable wing and thought, *Come to Mama!*

"How was your trip," she asked Marco a moment later, licking her lips and reaching for a second wing.

"Ah-mazing," he replied.

"Southeast Asia, right?"

He nodded. "Vietnam, Laos and Sri Lanka."

Chloe grinned. She loved hearing all about Marco's globe-trotting adventures as a professional photographer who shot limited-edition landscapes when he was not busy doing commissions for clients ranging from high-end fashion magazines to luxury travel properties.

"I can't wait to see your photos," she replied.

"You're coming to the opening next month, right."

"Of course!" she said, reaching for another wing. "I have it etched in stone on my calendar. By the way, I know I said this last time..."

"And the time before that," Marco chimed in with a smile.

"But this time I'm resolute. The next time you go overseas, we're coming with. You just have to give us enough heads up on when and where and we'll be there."

Jenna wrinkled her nose. "As long as it's First World."

"You're such a snob," Marco replied.

"I'm not a snob," Jenna retorted between chews. "I'm a New Yorker."

The night was cool and the moon shimmered at half-mast as Ian and Chloe stood side-by-side in the shorter of two lines that meandered towards an historic church, built in the late 1800s, that had been meticulously restored and transformed into a mixed-use performance space.

The entryway was decorated with illuminated

panels of stained glass that made one feel as though one was about to step into a sanctum.

About them stood New Yorkers of all shapes, stripes and styles, all eager to partake of Celeste's newest creation.

Ian glanced down at Chloe who seemed to be buzzing with anticipation by osmosis.

He was loving the low key sneakers she sported on her feet; and the easy, breezy way she had heeded his advice to dress comfortably. Some women he knew would have interpreted that as *wear three-inch heels instead of four-inch ones.*

His eye was then drawn to a delicate gold bracelet about her wrist that draped with charms of suns, moons and stars.

He reached out and touched one of the charms.

"Did you wear this because you had a premonition you were coming to a show called, Celeste?" he asked.

Chloe looked at the bracelet, loving the serendipity of it all.

"Celeste, huh," she said. "So the show has something to do with space or the heavens?"

"You'll see," he said with an air of mystery as he

took her hand in his, admiring the bracelet. "It's very pretty, where'd you get it?"

"My dad gave it to me for my birthday."

"Really? He has a good eye."

Chloe smiled. "I'm pretty sure my stepmom picked it out on his behalf."

"Behind every great man..." Ian said with a twinkle in his eye.

Reluctantly, he let go of her hand and retreated his own to a pants pocket.

"So do your parents know what you do for a living? Are they supportive?"

She nodded without hesitation. "They do. And yes, they are."

"Is your mom a matchmaker, too? Like, does this sort of thing run in the family?"

She shook her head. "Not with any of the generations I know about."

"Hmm," Ian said before he dived in deeper. "You're an only child right?"

She nodded.

"Are your parents at all worried that your work life may be interfering with your dating life?"

Chloe furrowed her brow. "What do you mean?"

He had not planned to go down a rabbit hole

of personal questions about her dating life, but damned if he did not want to know the answer to every last one of them. He told himself it had to do with his story; his readers would want to know Chloe the Matchmaker's dating status and relationship history.

"Well, you are here with me, a client, on a Saturday night, which is prime time in the dating world. I'd imagine that if you had a boyfriend, he wouldn't be too keen on you spending nights out with handsome, single men every weekend."

"Well, *if* I had a boyfriend, he would be someone who trusted that when I'm out with a client, male or female, handsome or otherwise, I'm one-hundred percent focused on helping them find their soulmate."

So, no boyfriend at the moment, Ian thought, filing that away... for his story.

"What about you? Have you met your soulmate yet?" he asked.

"Not yet," she said softly.

"Do you think you'll know it when you do?"

"Of course," she said with an upbeat smile.

But Ian was quick to notice her smile did not reach her eyes.

Could it be his magical matchmaker had an Achilles heel of her own? That her gift extended to all but herself; and she was just as mortal as the rest of us when it came to the affairs of her own heart?

"How can you be so certain?" he asked.

"My, aren't you rapid-fire with the questions tonight," she said with an exasperated grin.

"It's the reporter in me."

Chloe gave him a look. "What?"

Shit!

He suddenly realized the extent to which he had let down his guard around her.

"My friends say I fire off questions like a reporter," he replied, praying his attempted recovery was a graceful and believable one.

"Yeah, you kind of do," she replied.

"Okay, no more questions," he said as he pantomimed locking his lips and throwing away the key.

Chloe's eyes sparkled with amusement. "That's going to be hard for you, isn't it?"

He unlocked his lips. "You have no idea."

She giggled and he relished the melody of it as they drew nigh to the church's arch-shaped and intricately-carved wooden doors. He handed his VIP tickets to a young man wearing a blue vest.

"Enjoy the show," the man said.

Inside, the theatre's lobby was pulsing with the laughter and good cheer of couples and friends enjoying a pre-show cocktail.

"Do you want anything to eat? Drink?" Ian asked.

She shook her head. "I'm good."

"You sure?"

"I ate before I came. But please, don't let me stop you."

"What'd you eat?" he asked, guiding her to a set of doors leading into the main auditorium.

"Have you heard of K-Pow?"

Ian's mouth dropped.

"You had K-Pow and you didn't bring me any!" he said, melodramatically.

Chloe bit her lip. "*Mea culpa.*"

"Weeks ago, I bestowed upon you the divine gift of hourmet and all I get in return is *nada.*"

She grinned. "I promise, next time I have K-Pow before one of our sessions, I will bring you one."

"Just one?"

She breathed a guilty sigh. "You have *no idea* how quickly those things disappear in our house."

Ian laughed as they stepped into a dimly-lit auditorium that was spacious yet intimate. Spread out before them were rows of plush, microsuede loungers that reclined back 180-degrees if one so chose.

Ian glanced at Chloe who was staring at the loungers, not sure what to think.

"Um..." came the sound of her voice.

"I guess now's a good time to tell you the entire show takes place up there..." he said, pointing at the domed ceiling above.

"Ah," she breathed. "Hence the name, Celeste."

They weaved their way to a pair of VIP seats in the center of the room.

Moments later, once everyone had settled in their seats, the lights faded to black. As their eyes adjusted to the darkness, makeshift stars began to twinkle in the dome above.

Suddenly, an angelic nymph fluttered across the 'night sky,' gracefully, playfully.

Then another nymph appeared, and another and another till there were five. Orchestral music crescendoed about them as they danced and twirled and soared. Their every movement effortless. Mesmerizing. Beautiful.

Ian nestled his head back into the soft cushion of his seat, wondering if Chloe was as enthralled by the pomp and artistry of the opening sequence as he.

And, as the nymphs nosedived towards the audience then back up again, he knew this was shaping up to be Celeste's best show yet.

An hour later, when the lights shifted from dark to dim for intermission, Ian rolled his head to the right to look at Chloe.

She lay there, still staring up at the 'sky.' Her face was shadowed and he could not make out her expression.

"What'd you think?" he asked.

"That was amazing," she whispered.

She turned her head to meet his gaze. Her eyes glistened and Ian was struck by the wonderment in her eyes.

"Just... marvelous and amazing."

Ian smiled. "I'm glad you like it."

"Why have I never heard of this?"

"They're a traveling troupe that stops in the city

once or twice a year. They don't advertise, it's all word of mouth. Friends bringing friends. Girlfriends bringing boyfriends. They always sell out months in advance.

She grinned ever so sweetly. "Then I am doubly glad you brought me, because that was incredible. I've never seen anything like it."

"Me neither," he replied, thinking only of her.

A spell seemed to fall upon them as they gazed into each other's eyes, suddenly deaf to the words and blind to the movements of all those around them.

Ian noticed the remnants of a tear in the corner of her eye and reached over to wipe it away.

When his skin brushed against hers, her eyes fluttered, but she did not look away. Emboldened, Ian's touch gave way to a caress, as his thumb traced the contour of her cheek.

Like a moth to a flame, his gaze lowered to her lips and in that moment, he wanted nothing more than to savor the taste and feel of them.

He began to lean in for a kiss. His thumb caressing her cheek, his mind white hot with curiosity and desire.

"Ladies and gentlemen," came the sound of a

woman's voice on the PA system, "the performance will recommence in ten minutes."

Ian watched, powerless and with bated breath, as Chloe blinked and looked away, her mind switching back into work mode.

Reluctantly, his hand fell away from her face.

And just like that, the spell between them was broken.

ELEVEN

Chloe stalked through the front door of her apartment; tip-toed past Jenna and Marco who were cuddled up and fast asleep on the sofa; and continued onwards to her room where she fell face first into bed.

She buried her face in a pillow and muffled a scream.

What the hell was wrong with her? She had almost kissed a client.

A client.

A CLIENT!

Something she had never done or been tempted to do before.

She wanted to blame it on the romantic intimacy of the aerialist show. They had been lying next to each other, in the dark, shoulder to shoulder, for an hour before the forbidden kiss that almost was.

But she knew it probably had more to do with the glaring fact that she had been single for far too long. A problem she seriously needed to rectify by getting a Mr. Right Now, stat.

Because getting emotionally or physically involved with a client would be detrimental to her business, her reputation and, worse yet, her mission to bring star-crossed soulmates together.

She turned over, onto her back, and stared at the ceiling.

It would be best, she concluded, to hold off scheduling another session with Ian till she found someone suitable to have flirtatious – and kissable – nights o' fun with.

Because what had almost-happened hours before, could never, ever, *never* happen again.

"Ian..."
"Ian..."

"Earth to Ian."

Ian blinked and looked over at Fitz, who was trying to hand him an ice cold stein of beer.

"Thanks, man," he said taking the stein in hand.

"Why so deep in thought, in this of all places?" Fitz said looking down at the hallowed ground before them – a 94-foot long, maple wood court where the New York Knicks and the Miami Heat were battling it out to advance to the next round of the NBA Playoffs.

They were seated just three rows from the court. So close were they, Ian could see the contours of the sweat on each player's brow.

"I still can't get over how sweet these seats are," Ian said.

In truth, he had been lost in thought, replaying his almost-kiss with Chloe in his head. Over and over again.

"Tell me about it," Fitz replied. "And we owe it all to Chloe."

Ian furrowed his brow. "I thought Yuri gave you these tickets."

"Only because he's currently on a jet to St. Petersburg so Linda can meet his *babushka* in person."

Ian cocked a brow. "They've already advanced to meeting the babushka stage?"

"I don't know how things are going with this story of yours, but as far as I'm concerned, Chloe is a miracle worker. Before she matched up Linda and Yuri, Yuri was riding my ass, driving me *up the freakin' wall*. Now..."

"He's busy riding someone else," Ian interjected with a smirk.

Fitz grimaced and groaned, "Dude, I *do not* want to visualize Linda that way.... Ugh. Or Yuri!"

Ian laughed while Fitz took a pronounced gulp of beer, hoping to wash the thought away.

"But in all seriousness," Fitz said, his mind and palate cleansed. "Yuri's besotted and I've never seen Linda this happy. And it's all thanks to Chloe. How's she doing, by the way?"

"Chloe? She's good," Ian said, his mind flashing back to the way she had avoided his gaze after the show, when she bid him *adieu* and glided into a yellow cab.

He had not heard from or spoken to her since and he suddenly realized that she had yet to schedule their next session together. He really wished he could read what was going on in her mind right now.

Ian slid down in his seat and breathed a long, deep and silent sigh as he tried to focus on the action on the court.

Having grown up in the 'burbs of Boston, he and Fitz were both die-hard Celtics fans, so they were not rooting for either team in particular. But no one in their right mind would turn down free, third row tickets to a playoff game!

He watched as a referee called foul, and a Knicks player stepped up to the free-throw line. A hush fell over the stadium.

"We almost kissed," Ian said under his breath.

"We? Who?" Fitz's mouth dropped. "You and Chloe?"

Ian slow-nodded.

"Whoa. When?"

"Last Saturday."

The hometown crowd erupted with cheers but neither Ian nor Fitz were paying attention.

"Who almost kissed whom?"

Ian glanced at Fitz; the expression on his face said it all.

Fitz shook his head. "What a tangled web you weave, my friend." he said, taking a sip of beer.

"I know."

"Hey, I get it," Fitz said. "She's smart, beautiful, sweet…"

"She is. It's almost unbelievable how genuine she is. I mean, she matched up a Russian billionaire for free, expecting nothing in return as far as I can tell. She practically beams when she talks about couples she's brought together in the past. And she's so goddamn optimistic, it's damn near contagious.

"Is she seeing anyone?"

"No boyfriend at the moment."

Fitz's eyes brightened. "Ah. So what's the plan, Stan? With Chloe? With your story?"

Ian stared off into the distance, feeling completely lost and unmoored.

"I have no idea."

Chloe stepped out of the shower and put on her plush cotton robe, trying to decide whether she was going to wear her hair up or down for the night's festivities.

It had been two weeks since her almost-kiss with Ian, and she was getting ready for her first night out with Jenna as her wingwoman.

They were headed to *NY Woman's* Annual Summer's Eve Bash. The magazine's quarterly parties were always a fab mix of the best and brightest of New York's glitterati – from fashion to music; sports to politics; art to literature.

There was a good chance there would be a number of fun-loving bachelors in the mix for her to flirt with.

"Knock, knock," came the sound of Jenna's voice.

Chloe stepped out of her bathroom just as Jenna sashayed into her bedroom, carrying a trio of shopping bags from three different fashion houses.

"I come bearing gifts," Jenna said, channeling her inner dramatic actress.

"Gifts for what?"

"For you, silly."

Chloe glared. "You did not."

"I one hundred percent did."

"Jenna, I already picked out what I'm going to wear. It's cute, it's comfortable..."

Jenna wrinkled her nose.

"And I'm going to be putting it on right now," Chloe said, walking over to her closet.

"Yeah, no," Jenna retorted, pulling items from the bags and laying them out on the bed. "If you want me to be your wingwoman, then you have to adhere to my strict fashionista requirements. Non-negotiable."

Chloe glanced at the bed and frowned. "Are those stilettos?"

"You know it!" Jenna said with twinkle in her eye.

Then she looked at Chloe, cocked her head and put a hand on her hip.

"But first, we need to do something with your hair."

Two hours later, Chloe and Jenna stepped out of an elevator and onto the rooftop lounge of the swanky Illyia Hotel on Madison Avenue. Chloe was draped in a silky, golden dress that shimmered in the evening light. Wispy chandelier earrings twirled beneath her lobes. And, amazingly enough, the strappy stilettos on her feet were not as uncomfortable as she had feared.

She looked sexy. She felt sexy.

A look and a sensation she had not aspired to for a very long time.

She stood there for a moment, crowned by the glistening stars of the night sky, cloaked by the twinkling lights of the New York skyline, raring and ready to get her flirt on.

Yet another sensation she had not felt in a very long time.

"First things first," Jenna said, swiping a canapé from a roving waiter. "Open bar!"

They strutted over to a large, circular bar and ordered a pair of watermelon mojitos.

"So here's how it's going to go down," Jenna said, looking out at a sea of New York's hottest and brightest. "We're going to do a turn around the party. If you see someone you're interested in, let me know and I will make it happen. Ditto if I see someone you should be interested in."

The bartender returned with their drinks, which were topped with a sprig of mint and a spiraled slice of watermelon.

Jenna took a sip and moaned. "Oh my god, these things are manna from heaven."

She took another sip and breathed a different kind of moan. "Ooo, what about him?"

Chloe followed her line of sight to a guy with puppy dog eyes and a lopsided grin, who was leaning against the wall with his buddies, looking too cool for school.

"He's not even old enough to grow a beard," Chloe replied.

"Hey. You said you wanted light and fun. There's nothing more light and fun than a cutie in his early 20s who doesn't even know how to spell 'settle down' yet."

Chloe laughed then shook her head. "Hard pass."

"O-kay..." Jenna said, slowly panning her eyes about the room. "What about him?"

Chloe followed Jenna's line of sight once more... to a man on the other side of the bar who looked a lot like...

"That's Fitz," Chloe said softly and somewhat dazed.

"Who?"

"Ian's business partner."

Chloe realized she had yet to tell her best friend about her almost-kiss with Ian. Or her brunch not-date with Alexander.

She decided that, tomorrow, she would cook Jenna one of her rare yet delicious breakfasts; and catch her up on everything. The good, the bad and the *almost* scandalous.

"Ooo..." Jenna purred. "Another sexy architect. He's not a client of yours is he?"

"No. Why?"

"Because methinks he would make a perfect Mr. Right Now."

But Chloe's mind was elsewhere.

Her eyes moved about the room, hoping, praying, wishing that Fitz had come *hans solo* and Ian was somewhere, anywhere but here.

When her eyes landed back on Fitz, he had already spotted her and was making his way over, carrying a freshly-made Boston Sour in hand. He was wearing a dashing suit that screamed, *I may look like a GQ model, but there's so much more to me than that.*

He greeted her with the widest of grins and warmest of hugs.

"I don't know if you know this but you're top on my list of favorite people right now," he said.

Chloe could not help but smile. "Why's that?"

"Because you transformed my client from hell

into the best client ever. Before you, Yuri Petrovich was a pain in my derrière. In fact, I'm pretty sure I was on the fast track to getting an ulcer. Now he's so crazy in love, the other day, I started presenting a set of blueprints to him and you know what he said to me? He said…"

Fitz switched to a Russian accent – and a pretty good one at that. "Do want you think best. I trust your judgment."

He switched back to his normal voice. "Now, I'm really, really hoping that, when you say they're soulmates, that means they'll be together forever till death do they part."

"Trust me," Jenna said. "If Chloe says they're soulmates, then they're ride or die."

He breathed a contented sigh of relief. "I'm Fitz, by the way," he said, reaching out to shake Jenna's hand.

Chloe grimaced at her slip in manners. "Fitz, this is my friend, Jenna. Jenna, this is Fitz, he's a commercial architect."

"I do residential as well," he said, pulling out his wallet and handing Jenna a card.

"A jack of all architectural trades," Jenna said, taking the card and giving Chloe a wink that loosely translated to: *He's hot, successful and has good taste in clothes and liquor. Girl, you better reel him in!*

"So Fitz," Jenna continued, morphing into sleuth mode. "Are you here by yourself, or..."

Suddenly, Jenna's clutch rattled on the bar counter.

"Excuse me," she said, pulling out her vibrating phone. "Hey, babe, can you hear me? You here yet...?"

She began to walk away in search of a quieter spot.

Chloe turned her attention back to Fitz, who was looking over her shoulder.

"Speaking of which," he said, "here comes my plus-one."

Chloe's shoulders stiffened. She really hoped he was referring to a girlfriend... though a girlfriend had never come up when she had had lunch with him and Ian at a steakhouse near the construction site. Yet, a couple of weeks had passed since then, so maybe, just maybe, Fitz had met someone.

Chloe turned her head and was surprised-not-surprised to see Ian walking towards them. He was rocking the same ensemble he had worn during their first session together. His dry cleaner had done an exemplary job removing the dirt and coffee stains from his crisp white button-up.

Their eyes locked and Ian blinked with surprise.

"Hey," he said softly upon approach.

"Hi," she replied, greeting him with the warmest smile she could muster.

She made an impromptu decision to play it totally and completely cool. As if their almost-kiss had never happened. As if she had not been deliberately avoiding him till she got her hormones in check and focused on someone who was not a client. Which was what tonight was supposed to be about... before Ian showed up.

With any luck, he too would pretend nothing had almost-happened between them. Then things could go back to normal and she could continue on her contractual quest to find his soulmate.

"I didn't know you were a *NY Woman* kind of guy," she said teasingly, trying to lighten the mood.

"Fitz makes it a point to network once or twice a month, it helps him find new clients."

Chloe looked back at Fitz to find he had already been pulled away by a divorcee to whom he was giving his business card; but it was clear she was desirous of more than just his architectural prowess.

"What about you?" Ian asked, sliding his hands in his pockets. "What brings you here?"

"I came with Jenna," she said glancing at her best friend, who was by the elevators, greeting a well-dressed Marco with a lovey-dovey kiss.

"Ah, and is that her soulmate, perchance?"

Chloe smiled. "It is."

"So another match made by Chloe?"

She looked at him and nodded.

He stared at her for a moment, saying nothing. Then...

"There's something I need to talk to you about," he said, his voice somber. "Mind if we go somewhere quieter?"

Chloe inwardly groaned. *So much for pretending.*

"Sure," she said, reluctantly.

The last thing she wanted was for this whole awkward situation to get even more awkward. She had a feeling this 'talk' was going to be a hefty one. Hefty as in he either wanted to address the elephant in the room. Or, worse...

He wanted to fire her.

Ian held the elevator door open as Chloe stepped inside. Then he moved to stand beside her and the door slid shut, leaving them alone and in silence.

Ian glanced at Chloe who was lost in thought. He could tell she was nervous, though she hid it well.

He wondered what she was nervous about. What she was expecting him to say, seeing how he was not even sure what he was going to say just yet.

He was still reeling from the coincidence that of all the parties in Manhattan and beyond, they had ended up at the same one.

He was also having trouble concentrating, given that sexy, golden dress of hers that clung to her curves like honey. Her lips were glossy red, her hair a cathedral of curls atop her head, and her legs... god her legs...

A ping sounded and the elevator door opened up to the lobby.

Ian had been to this hotel before, to meet with a source, a corporate whistleblower. He knew there was a garden terrace at the far end of the hotel that would be quiet and private this time of night.

He guided Chloe down a long hallway to a pair of gilded French doors.

They stepped out onto the terrace. An oceanic breeze fluttered the leaves of the trees and the scent of jasmine hung lightly in the air. Ian closed the door behind him and turned to face Chloe.

"Are you cold?" he asked.

"I'm good," she replied with a shake of the head.

He cleared his throat. "So, the thing I wanted to talk to you about... is..."

He gazed upon her face, which looked angelic in the moonlight. He gazed into her eyes, which wavered with concern and fearful anticipation.

"I'd like to put an end to our contract," he said at long last.

"Oh," she said sadly. "May I ask why?"

"I've met someone... I think."

"That's great," she said with measured enthusiasm.

Ian looked up at the heavens and breathed a long, deep sigh.

"What's wrong?" Chloe asked.

He raked his fingers through his hair, trying to shore up the courage to say what he wanted to say.

"Is she married?" she asked, filling the silence between them.

He shook his head.

"Is she a client of yours?"

"In a... sense."

"Oh, okay, well, we could schedule a time for me to see her discreetly so you can know for certain, if you'd like."

His eyes connected with hers. "What if certainty's not an option?"

She cocked her head, not quite following.

He took a step towards her, hands in his pockets, willing himself to stay the course despite the orchestral pounding of his heart.

"This woman I'm interested in... the weekend before last, I sat beside her in a theatre, under a ceiling of celestial stars and we almost, almost kissed. I haven't been able to think of anything else since."

He gazed deep into her eyes and watched as realization dawned upon her face.

"Ian..." She closed her eyes and slowly shook her head. "You're my client..."

"Ex-client, as of just a moment ago."

She stared back at him, at an utter and complete loss for words.

"Before you say anything... I know this isn't something either of us planned. But when I'm with you, I feel...

He racked his brain for the just-right word.

"I am in awe of you, Chloe. I love the way you are... with me, with other people, when you think no one's watching. I feel like there's this connection between us and it's taken me by surprise probably as much as I'm taking you by surprise right now."

Her eyes fell away from him, but still, he stayed the course.

"But this thing, this something between us, I can't stop thinking that maybe, just maybe, it could be the very thing we've both been searching for. I'd really like to see if it is and I'm hoping you do too. I think we owe it to ourselves to find out.

Chloe's eyes remained trained on the ground. She was quiet and still. Which gave Ian a glimmer of hope. Was her silence a sign of indecision? Was there a chance his heartfelt words were not falling on deaf ears?

He reached for her hands and laced his fingers with hers.

Chloe flinched and closed her eyes, but still he stayed the course.

"Have dinner with me..." he said softly.

She bit the bottom corner of her lip.

"Tomorrow night. You like seafood?"

Seconds passed, then slowly, ever so slowly, she nodded.

Ian smiled. "I'll pick you up at six."

Her gaze lifted to his and he could see angels of Doubt and Curiosity warring in her eyes.

"You won't regret it, I promise," he said with a reassuring grin. "If it works out between us, if it doesn't work out between us, one way or another we'll know."

He gazed deep into her eyes, fighting the urge to kiss her right then and there.

"But I have a really good feeling that this, all of this, is happening for a reason."

TWELVE

The next morning, Chloe awoke feeling dazed and confused.

Last night had not gone as planned. At all. Instead of leaving the party with a Mr. Right Now on deck, she had left with a personal and professional dilemma on her hands.

She felt like she was wading in deep and unchartered waters. Never had she imagined or contemplated that a client... or ex-client... would ask her out on a date. She did not even know where that fell on the ethical line.

She supposed the *ex-client* part made it more kosher. And it was not as if she had come onto Ian.

Outside of their almost-kiss, she had always been professional around him.

Well, excepting those brief, few seconds when she had stared at his nearly-nude physique in the pool. A physique, mind you, that had definitely lived up to Jenna's moniker: *Mr. Sexy Architect.*

Now, here she was, less than ten hours away from going out with him on an actual date. And she was not yet sure how she felt about that... or him, for that matter.

Last night, she had experienced just how intoxicating and persuasive confidence could be. The sheer strength of Ian's belief that there was something between them worth exploring had swayed her into saying yes.

She could not deny that, compared to previous clients, things had been different with him since day one... since that moment on the train when he had curbed her fall and pulled her in close, his arm around her waist, the masculine warmth of his breath upon her face.

She did not allow herself to think anything of it at the time.

Just as she did not allow herself to think anything of the jolt of electricity she had felt whilst standing on the edge of the pool as he gazed up at her with those soulful eyes of his.

Instead, she had chalked it up to being single and bereft of romance for far too long.

Just as she had chalked up his revolving door of personal questions about her life, her family, her likes and dislikes as being nothing more than a facet of his personality, that he was just naturally inquisitive – albeit way more inquisitive than any other client before him.

So maybe he was right, maybe there was something there, between them. But that did not necessarily mean they were soulmates. And therein lay the bigger question and the biggest dilemma of all:

Was she willing to dive into a relationship with a man who may not be her soulmate?

Having a summer fling with a Mr. Right Now, that she was comfortable with. She could gird her heart from falling in love with a guy who was non-committal and just looking to have fun.

But Ian was not looking for a summer fling. Though he had put an end to their contract, he was still a man in search of his soulmate. He wanted a love and a relationship that was serious and everlasting.

As did she.

Was she willing to risk potentially falling in love with him, or him with her, when there was a fifty-fifty chance they were not meant to be, in the long-term?

Hoping to clear her mind and hone her thoughts, Chloe suited up, hopped on the subway and went for a 10-mile run across the Brooklyn Bridge and further on along a waterfront trail. As she stared out at the waves of the sea, she thought back on her relationship with Greg, her ex.

Greg was handsome and driven like Ian, like Alexander.

He was also a complexity of thoughtfulness, intelligence, charm, pomposity, self-absorption and being much too obsessed with keeping up appearances.

But he adored her and she him.

They were together for three fun years before he dropped down on one knee on a cool autumn day in Martha's Vineyard and asked for her hand in marriage.

Caught up in the emotions of being proposed to by the man she loved, Chloe said yes.

Hours later, however, in the quiet of the night, she had lain awake, deeply concerned that she still was not one hundred percent certain Greg was The One. She prayed Fate would give her a definitive sign before she said, 'I do.'

Four months into their engagement, Chloe was on the cusp of resigning from Werner + Ball to focus on matchmaking full-time. This was something she had discussed with Greg on several occasions prior to their engagement; something he seemed to fully support.

They were out to dinner one night, catching up on each other's weeks, when she beamed an elated smile and shared that she had just finished drafting her resignation letter and planned to hand it to her boss the following Monday.

Greg smiled back approvingly. "That's great! It'll give you more time to focus on the wedding and house hunting."

"Well, a *little* more time," she replied. "I'm going to be pretty swamped with my backlog of clients.

Thankfully, we have an awesome wedding planner and Jenna's boss recommended a really good realtor, so I plan on leaving most of it in their capable hands."

"Swamped with clients?" Greg said, not following.

"Matchmaking clients."

He stared at her for a moment. "You're serious?"

"What?"

"I thought you were quitting your job so you could focus on the wedding and starting a family together."

Chloe stared back at him, flabbergasted. "I never said that."

"Greg," she said, dropping her voice to an impatient whisper. I've been talking about expanding my business for nearly a year now. I thought you were behind me on this."

"That was before we got engaged. You know how important starting a family is to me. To us."

"That doesn't mean we have to start one right away. We're both focused on building our careers right now. I'm not giving that up the moment we say, 'I do.'"

In the past, they had discussed having kids – she

wanted two, he wanted three or four – but they had never discussed a timeline or the sacrifices each of them would have to make when they became parents.

Such was the underlying issue with their relationship. They liked being together, spending time with one another, doing thoughtful little things to make the other person feel special.

But when it came to deeper topics and issues, they would dance over the depths like dragonflies.

Truth was, they both wanted to maintain a happy-go-lucky relationship, free from the conflicts and squabbles that weighed down other couples. Sure, they would have disagreements from time to time, but they would always kiss and make up within the hour, conceding that both of them were right... and wrong.

"Chlo," Greg said, leaning forward. "You know I love you and adore you. But let's be honest here, playing matchmaker isn't a career. Its a hobby. I always thought you were doing it just for fun."

"I'm not doing it just for fun, I'm doing it because it's my calling."

Greg closed his eyes and slowly shook his head, as

though he was speaking to a child who still believed in Santa Claus.

"Greg," she said, laying her knife and fork on the starch white tablecloth. "Do you believe I have a gift; that I can see when two people are meant to be together?"

"I always thought that was whimsically ingenious marketing on your part," he said, with sincerity and a smile.

Greg picked up his fork and cut into a flaky filet of salmon.

"Look I'm not saying you have to give up matchmaking completely," he continued. "I just don't think we should push back on starting a family for something you can easily do in your spare time."

Chloe sat there and stared at Greg, confronted with the painful realization that her fiancé, the man she was planning to spend the rest of her life with, did not believe in the cornerstone that defined who she was and guided her purpose in life.

And that's when she knew, without a shadow of a doubt, that Greg was not her soulmate.

The next day, heartbroken and in tears, she called off the engagement. Jenna returned the ring on her behalf, as Chloe mourned the end of a relationship that had been a significant part of her twenties.

Greg had tried, numerous times, to get her to change her mind. Wanting very much for them to kiss and make up. Like they always did.

Yet, despite the gut-wrenching heartbreak, she knew there was no turning back. Fate had answered her prayers; and Chloe knew it would be folly to ignore it.

At the time, she had been too melancholy with grief over the breakup to notice that Fate had quietly added a box to her *Is He The One?* checklist. Namely that her soulmate would be someone who believed in and championed her gift.

Ian was already a client of hers... well, ex-client... so he already trusted her skills as a gifted matchmaker. Plus, he easily checked off a number of other boxes. He was smart, handsome, thoughtful, adventurous and fun to be around.

They had an easy rapport – that alone was worth its weight in gold.

And, given their almost-kiss, there was no denying there was chemistry between them.

By the time she made it back to the stoop of her apartment building, Chloe had reached a decision.

She would not renege on her date with Ian. Instead, she would do what she had done once before... she would trust in *Auntie Fate*, as Brad would say.

She lifted her eyes to the heavens and prayed that if Ian was not The One, *Her One*, Fate would grace her with knowledge and illumination before she fell too far down the emotional rabbit hole.

Till then, she had a date to get ready for.

Hours later, showered, dressed and freshly perfumed, Chloe made her way back down to the stoop, where Ian was leaning on a balustrade, waiting for her. He was dressed casual and cool in a pair of dark, pressed jeans; a Nirvana smiley face t-shirt; and a blue suede blazer.

A yellow cab idled on the street behind him.

The moment he saw her, his eyes brightened. No doubt, he had been looking forward to this all day.

"Hey, beautiful," he said, taking in the periwinkle chiffon of her dress and the silvery shimmer of her ballet flats.

"Hi," she replied, her voice soft and nervous.

She was used to interacting with Ian on a

professional level. Now the energy and the vibe between them was different. The matchmaker-client wall was down, and she had no idea how to be completely casual around him.

In fact, she felt as though she had just stepped into a parallel dimension wherein much was the same, yet there were enough differences and nuances to keep her on her toes.

"There's one thing I need to say before we go," she said.

"Okay," he replied, staring up at her as though he had all the time in the world.

"I want you to promise me that, if things don't pan out between us, we will pick up where we left off and resume the search for your soulmate."

"Well, I have a very good feeling that won't be necessary," he said with quiet confidence. Then his lips spread into a slow grin. "But yes, I promise and agree to those terms."

She stared into his eyes, looking for some semblance of worry or doubt on his part. But the energy in his gaze was calm and reassuring, like a safe harbor.

"Okay," she breathed, glad to have gotten that out of the way.

"Ready?" he asked, reaching for her hand as though he was Lancelot and she his Guinevere.

She smiled back and laced her fingers with his. "Ready."

Their first stop was a *nouveau* comedy club. Chloe had a feeling Ian had chosen the place in hopes of easing her nerves and easing their way into the date.

"This is one of my favorite places in the city," he said during the cab ride over. "It's a pop-up comedy club that takes place in the courtyard of this guy's apartment building every week when the weather's good. They only have one rule: no lazy jokes allowed. No fat jokes. No race jokes. No gay jokes, sexist jokes, yo momma jokes..."

"No yo momma jokes!" Chloe interjected, feigning mock outrage.

Ian chuckled. "And no making fun of people in the audience unless they heckle you first."

"I like it," Chloe said with a nod. "I hate when comedians make fun of people. I'm like, are we back in high school?"

"Exactly. These guys and gals, they have to be

smart. They have to be clever and original. When they're on point, they spin out jokes and witticisms and social commentary that makes you laugh and think and reflect all at the same time."

"I'm looking forward to it," Chloe said with a grin of anticipation. She rarely went to comedy clubs and had never been to one so avant-garde.

"Now, I should warn you, the comics are encouraged to try out new material and sometimes a few of them bomb really bad, like gloriously, flamingly bad. But I admire that," he said, still holding fast to her hand. "Amongst all the art forms, I think standup comedy is the most fearless. It's just you and the audience. And the audience is just sitting there, in judgment, ready to crucify you if you don't make them laugh."

"You sound like you speak from experience," Chloe said.

He shook his head and chuckled. "I know my short list of talents, and standup isn't one of them. But I did take a few improv classes when I first moved to New York."

"Really!"

He nodded. "It's like bungee jumping off a bridge. Terrifying and exhilarating and really freeing.

Taking improv made me much more fearless when it came to my career and the demands of the job. I think it's partly the secret to my success."

"*The Improvisational Architect*," she said with a twinkle in her eye. "That would be an intriguing book title if you ever feel compelled to write one."

He looked at her for a long moment, then averted his gaze to the window.

"Yeah, it would," he said, his voice low, almost somber.

Chloe wondered why his mood had shifted all of a sudden. Had she touched a nerve? Was he secretly a failed novelist or something? He did have a remarkable way with words, so she would not be surprised if he had a couple of unpublished or unfinished manuscripts stuffed in a drawer somewhere.

When they arrived at the comedy club, they grabbed a pair of beers and a bowl of chips and salsa, then commandeered two Adirondack lawn chairs near the makeshift stage. Around forty people milled about, from all walks of New York life. Rows of globular string lights danced in the gentle breeze above their heads. Super chill Caribbean music played from a set of speakers nearby.

By the time the MC took the stage to welcome everyone to his humble, outdoor abode, Chloe was feeling zen and *irie*.

Life is good, she thought to herself as she turned her head and smiled at Ian. His eyes smiled back at her, pleased that she was enjoying herself thus far.

Just as Ian had foreshadowed, the show was funny in refreshing and original ways. A few of the sets did, indeed, turn out to be glorious bombs. But, in the spirit of good fun and artful comradery, the MC ended up giving a free kamikaze shot to each such comic before they stepped off-stage, along with an open invitation to come back next time.

"Joan Rivers once said," the MC shared at the close of the show, "'my whole career has been one rejection after another, and then going back and pushing against everything and everybody. Getting ahead by small, ugly steps.' Whether you're a comedian, artist, actor, writer, activist, civil engineer, or whatever, never give up on your dream of making a difference on this great, big, beautiful world of ours. Till next time, *namaste*."

As people began to mill out, Chloe followed Ian as he walked up to a huddle of beer-guzzling comedians and gave them kudos and props for putting a great show.

Back outside, on the sidewalk, Ian took her by the hand and they walked two blocks to Pampas, a lovely, Latin fusion restaurant brimming with the colors and flavors of South America. They ordered an assortment of tapas, a glass of Argentinian Malbec for her, and a bottle of Mexican *cerveza* for him.

"I figured this place would pair nicely with your audiobook," he said, as candlelight flickered on the table between them. "Have you finished it yet?"

"I did," she replied.

She did not have much free time to read books in print form, but she had recently discovered that she quite liked listening to audiobooks while she was getting ready in the morning.

"So did all three of them make it out alive? And if not, was an anaconda involved in one way or another?"

Chloe laughed. "Thankfully, they're all alive. But one of them is still there, married to a tribesman."

"Really?" Ian said with a cock of the brow. "That's quite the adjustment."

He took a swig of beer.

"Could you do that?" he asked. "Live in a completely different culture with a completely different way of life?"

"I don't know. I've never thought about it. Could you?"

"Hell no," he said jovially. Then he thought about it and shrugged. "I mean, I could probably do it for a couple months. Then the patina would wear off and I'd be back here in the USA, drinking overpriced beer and binge watching bad TV shows."

Chloe chuckled. "The American way."

"Ya damn right," Ian drawled like a gun-toting, tobacco-chewing cowboy of the Wild West.

The more the conversation flowed between them, the more Chloe relaxed. By the time they ordered dessert, she felt like she had found her casual stride with Ian. It certainly helped that he was witty and a great conversationalist.

While dessert was en route, Chloe stole away to the ladies room. When she emerged from a stall and walked over to a Spanish-tiled alcove to wash her hands, she smiled at an older lady in her seventies who was standing in front of a mirror, putting on a fresh coat of blush lipstick.

The lady smiled back and Chloe was struck by

the youthfulness of her gaze. She looked like a woman who had thoroughly enjoyed every single one of her seventy-plus years.

"How are you tonight, my dear," the woman asked, her voice cultured and proper, like an Englishwoman who had been in the States for a very long time.

"I'm good and you?" Chloe replied. She always had a soft spot for senior citizens. She admired their grace, wit and wisdom. And, of course, they reminded her of her grandparents, whom she adored.

"Oh I'm just fine, my dear. Just fine. I saw you out there...," she said, nodding at the door leading back to the dining room, "having a grand old time with your beau."

Chloe smiled. *Beau.* She was pretty sure she had never heard that word outside the confines of a black-and-white movie classic.

"The pair of you make a lovely couple. What does he do, if you don't mind me asking?"

"He's an architect."

The woman's eyes alighted with surprise. "An architect? Now that's a rare and noble profession.

One doesn't run into one of those every day. How did you meet?"

Chloe thought back to where it all began. "At the gym."

"Ah, well that is a plus. You both care about your health. I always tell my children, your health is your wealth."

Chloe nodded. She had never heard that expression before, but she whole-heartedly agreed. Luckily, constantly being on-the-go – meeting with clients and, on occasion, chasing after clueless soulmates – helped her stay in pretty good shape.

"How many children do you have?" Chloe asked.

"Two. A boy and a girl. Or I should say, a forty-two-year-old man and a thirty-six-year-old woman."

"Do they live close by?"

"Amy does. Peter's in Seattle with his wife and my precious granddaughter, Lola," she said with the widest of grins. "She's four."

Chloe's eyes smiled. For many retired parents, there was no greater joy than the gift of grandchildren.

"You and your beau... what's his name?" the woman asked.

"Ian."

"You and Ian, how long have you been courting?"

Courting. Chloe just loved how sweet and old-fashioned that sounded.

"It's our first date," she replied.

The woman gasped with delight. "Oh, I never would've guessed! The two of you have such lovely rapport."

"We've known each other for a while."

"Ah, friends first. That, my dear, is the secret to a long and happy marriage," the woman said with a wag of a silk-gloved finger.

That was something Chloe had heard before. Whenever she encountered a happy couple who had been together for twenty-plus years, she always asked what was the secret to their success. Nine times out of ten, they would say something to the effect of, 'I married my best friend.'

"Well it was lovely talking to you, my dear," the woman said, heading for the door. "Enjoy the rest of your date."

Chloe bid her farewell then turned back to the mirror. She adjusted her hair, glided on a fresh coat of lip gloss, then made her way back to the dining area.

Her gaze landed on Ian, whose back was to her. His eyes were trained on a delectable chocolate dish holding court in the middle of the table. He had left the dessert untouched, awaiting her return.

Suddenly she blinked.

Then blinked again.

Then blinked once more... as the thread of kismet wound its way around Ian's shoulders.

Her mouth dropped.

No freaking way!

Her eyes followed the thread to the other side of the room where the older lady she had been speaking with just moments before stood in front of coat check, buttoning up a designer jacket that was vintage to others, but original to her.

The thread of kismet fell gracefully upon her shoulders, like a magical shawl.

Okay, this is crazy, Chloe thought as her mind shifted into overdrive.

She glanced back at Ian, then whipped her gaze back over to the old woman, who had disappeared through the front door.

Chloe bolted past tables and waiters and busboys to the front of the restaurant and arrived just in time to see the woman's gloved hand closing the door of a towncar before it drove off.

Chloe looked to her left then her right and dashed over to a yellow cab that had just dropped off a couple in their late fifties. She dived into the backseat and, without skipping a beat, pointed at the towncar in the distance.

"Not to sound like a movie cliché, but... can you follow that black car?"

"The towncar?" the cabbie asked, not the least bit fazed by the request.

"Yes, please," she replied, her heart pounding.

Her gift was something she never questioned, but here she was chasing after an elderly woman and even she thought it was crazy. It made no sense whatsoever that Ian... *her 3-hour beau...* was destined to be with a woman over twice his age.

Maybe her gift was evolving. Maybe the line of kismet was leading her to the woman's daughter or niece or age-appropriate neighbor.

In the absence of any definitive answers, all she could do was focus on the task at hand – not losing sight of the old woman. She kept her eyes peeled on the towncar, serving as a second set of eyes in case the cabbie blinked the wrong way and lost sight of his mark.

For a brief moment, her mind flashed to Ian, of what he must be thinking and feeling in the wake of her prolonged absence. She knew she should text him, but she could not risk looking away from the towncar, not even for a split second.

Instead, she fished her phone out of her purse and voice dialed his number.

"Hey, is everything okay?" he asked without missing a beat. She could hear a mixed bag of emotions in his voice: worry, disappointment, relief, hope...

"Yes. Something really urgent has come up. I'm so sorry I had to leave in a hurry, I promise I'll explain later."

Her heart caught in her throat as the towncar sailed through a yellow light just as it turned red. Luckily, the cabbie was thoroughly motivated by the adrenaline rush and the unspoken promise of a great tip, and he proceeded to gun it across the intersection.

"Where are you?" Ian asked.

"In a cab," she said honestly, without thinking.

"Are you on autopilot?"

"What?" she said, not following.

"You said you go on autopilot when you see two soulmates who aren't together, in the same vicinity."

"Yeah, I do..." she mumbled, her eyes glued to the red taillights as the towncar turned left onto a narrow street. The cabbie had to wait for three damnable cars to pass before he could follow in pursuit.

Ian chuckled. "I can tell you're on autopilot right now. Is there anything I can do to help?"

"No... not yet, at least," she replied, briefly wondering how she would break the news to him later on – that the person she had been chasing was, in fact, his soulmate... in a seven-degrees-of-separation kind of way, she imagined.

"Okay, well, call me if you need anything. I'll be on standby."

"I will. Thanks."

She hung up and tossed the phone back into her purse.

Moments later, the towncar pulled into the circular driveway of an upscale apartment building; and slowed to a stop under a royal blue awning.

A doorman wearing a Pullman-style cap stepped forward and opened the passenger-side door.

Out stepped a young woman with a glorious and fiery mane of hair and a forest green wrap dress draped around her vivacious curves. In her right hand, she carried an oversized and overstuffed, white leather tote bag with a grey wig peaking out over the top.

As the woman sashayed down a royal blue runner to the building's glass-paneled entrance, Chloe's mind swirled with recognition and the realization that the old woman with the youthful eyes she had been talking to in the Pampas ladies room... the woman who was destined to be the love of Ian's life... was none other than the illustrious Vikki Hot Lips herself.

THIRTEEN

"No fucking way!" Jenna gasped.

Chloe poured another helping of Shirley Temple with a twist into her martini glass.

The twist being a double shot of vodka.

Chloe was not one to drink alcohol outside of social occasions, but after the night she had had...

"You've got to be kidding me?" Jenna exclaimed, sitting across from her on the sofa. "Vikki Hot Lips and Mr. Sexy Architect?"

"Yep."

"And this happened while the two of you were on a date?"

Chloe took a long gulp of the bubbly elixir then nodded.

"Wow. So, temporarily ignoring the fact that I'm just finding out about this date of yours *after the fact*, how do you feel?"

"I feel... numb," she said, as four shots of vodka were already in the throes of working their magic. "Totally, completely, delightfully numb.... I mean, don't get me wrong, I'm happy for him, I really am. And for me too, because now I know, without a shadow of a doubt, he's not my soulmate."

"Yeah, but what a way to find out."

Chloe's eyes bulged in agreement.

"I didn't even know you were interested in Ian like that."

"Well, he was a client so I wasn't interested. But one would be blind not to notice he has a wit and an energy that's attractive, endearing..."

"Plus, he's super hot," Jenna added for good measure.

Chloe giggled. "That too. But I didn't even contemplate him in the romantic sense till he asked me out, in earnest. And then I figured, why not? What if, in the end, I had more to gain than to lose?"

"Hold up, did I hear you correctly? Did you just

say you were willing to take a *romantic risk* with Ian?"

Chloe responded with a slow, intoxicated nod.

"Ooo, my little Chlo's growing up," Jenna replied with a melodramatic sniffle.

Chloe rolled her eyes. "Much good it did me, seeing how I'm right back where I started: single with zero prospects."

"That would be true *if* you lived in a universe where Alexander Turin didn't exist."

"Alexander's a bust," she said, tossing back the last of her Shirley Temple.

Jenna rolled her eyes. "Here we go..."

"No, seriously, I had brunch with him the other day."

"W-h-a-t!" Jenna wrapped a hand around the nearest throw pillow and threw it at Chloe's head. "Why am I just now hearing about this?"

"I've been busy," Chloe said lamely.

"You didn't tell me about your date with Ian. You didn't tell me about your date with Alexander..." A wave of hurt washed across Jenna's face. "Did I do something wrong? We used to tell each other everything."

"No, you didn't...." Chloe leaned her head back

on the cushion and breathed a deep, long sigh. "I just needed to figure some things out on my own."

"I get it. I can be uber-ly and vocally opinionated sometimes," Jenna said somberly.

"Sometimes?" Chloe replied, cocking a brow.

Jenna chuckled.

Chloe reached for her hand. "Honestly, I love that you're opinionated and you care enough to shower me with your advice, even when I need it but don't want to hear it."

"I just want you to be happy," Jenna replied, squeezing Chloe's hand.

Chloe smiled. "I know."

"So..." Jenna said, her eyes brimming with excitement. "Tell me about your date with Alexander."

"It wasn't a date, it was a friendly brunch..."

"Yadda, yadda, yadda."

"There isn't much to tell. The brunch was nice. Really nice. We talked. Caught up. Then he brought me home, gave me a hug and drove off."

"Just a hug?"

"Just a hug."

"No kiss?"

Chloe shook her head.

"Not even on the cheek?"

"Well, he always does that."

"Did you want him to kiss you?"

"No," Chloe said... a little too quickly.

Jenna squinted her eyes and pursed her lips. "Oh the lies that spill forth from your lips when you speak of Alexander. What's the last thing he said to you?"

"We should do this again sometime."

"That's it?"

Chloe nodded.

"Those were his exact words?"

"To the letter."

"Hmm...." Jenna pursed her lips, lost in thought.

"So, you see, I was right all along. Alexander's feelings for me are purely platonic. Always have been. Always will be. So now you can put your theories to rest and..."

"I don't know, sometimes you don't hear very well."

"Like when?"

"Or... maybe he didn't want to toss out a specific date because he travels a lot and didn't want to cancel on you."

"If that was the case, then he would've said, 'let's do this again when I'm back in town.'"

Jenna snapped her fingers and sat up on her knees. "No. You know what it is... he's having an impossible time gaging where you're at."

"What's that supposed to mean?"

"Answer me this, if Alexander called you right now and asked you out to dinner, what would you say?"

Chloe's mouth dipped into a frown. "I don't know."

"See, that's my point. He doesn't know where he stands with you because you still haven't come to terms with how you feel about him. He probably drove away from that date thinking *you* still had him squarely in the friendzone."

Chloe breathed a deep sigh as she lay her head back and closed her eyes. "You're never going to drop this are you?"

"Nope. Never.... Unless and until you get definitive proof he isn't your soulmate, like you did with Ian tonight."

"I'll get right on that," Chloe mumbled as she began to drift on a soft, white cloud, en route to a fabulous land where all of life's problems were naught but a dream.

The next morning, Chloe awoke hangover free yet fully dreading the day ahead. Not because she did not want to connect Ian with his true-blue soulmate. She did.

She just had a strong feeling this was going to be her trickiest match-up yet; and she was not entirely sure she was up for the challenge. In truth, all she really wanted to do was stay in bed all day... and all night.

Unfortunately, though, she did not have the luxury of time. She had to speak to Vikki before Ms. Hot Lips published whatever story she was working on; assuming she had not already done so.

If Chloe had not been in total and complete shock the night before, she would have figured out a way to talk to Vikki right then and there, to preempt the publication of a story featuring her or Ian. She prayed Vikki had been too tired from pretending to be an elderly grandmother to send anything to a late-night editor. Not just for the sake of Chloe's reputation, but also because she knew Ian would be even less open to being with Vikki if he ended up being the butt of one of her exposés.

Hey, so I put your life on blast to millions of people. Want to spend the rest of your life with me?

Chloe knew that, for Ian, the answer would be an unequivocal no.

Once the vodka had worn off, Chloe had tossed and turned all through the night, trying to figure out why the City's most illustrious gossip columnist had donned a disguise just to talk to her. Was she looking for dirt on the woman she had recently declared, *The Hottest Matchmaker in Manhattan?* Did she know Ian was Chloe's client... well, *former* client?

And if so, was she planning to publicly question Chloe's integrity and ethics, to the *schadenfreude* of a million-plus readers?

Despite the dictum, *don't believe everything you hear*, when it came to gossip, most people were hard-pressed not to do just that – especially when it spilled forth from the pen of Vikki Hot Lips. Chloe shuddered to think of the damage such an exposé would have on her business and reputation.

Reluctantly, she rolled out of bed, shuffled to her

desk, opened the laptop and went directly to Vikki's column on the *New York Metro's* website. She breathed a sigh of relief when she saw that the top story was an exclusive bombshell on a married talk show host who had been touting family values to the masses... whilst secretly *sugar daddying* college-aged mistresses for years.

Chloe closed the laptop and unlocked her cell phone.

It was time to call in a favor.

FOURTEEN

Chloe stepped into the atrium of the *New York Metro's* downtown headquarters. She was clad in a power suit and three-inch heels from her consulting days. Reputedly, Vikki Hot Lips was a force to be reckoned with, and Chloe wanted to make sure Vikki knew she was no shrinking violet herself.

She checked in at the security desk, where a name badge was waiting for her thanks to a former client who sat on the *Metro's* board of directors; then she rode an elevator to the twenty-second floor. When the doors glided open, she was greeted by the sights and sounds of a big city newsroom. The building itself had served as the Metro's headquarters for seventy-plus years and she swore she could smell typewriter ink lingering from a bygone era.

The newsroom was abuzz with energy and urgency as reporters, editors and photographers typed, talked, run-walked, edited, laughed, argued and downed copious amounts of coffee.

The man at the security desk had told her Vikki's office would be at the rear of the building.

"Just look out for a big ole pair of red lips," he had said with a glint in his eye.

Chloe was not entirely sure if he was referring to Vikki's actual lips or something else entirely. Yet, as she made her way down a corridor to the other side of the building, in the distance, she spied an oversized decal of ruby red lips hanging on a wall.

Bingo!

Chloe followed the *yellow brick road* to Vikki's office, where Vikki sat behind a glass desk, typing up her next exposé.

Hopefully one that isn't about me, Chloe thought.

She squared her shoulders and knocked on the door.

Vikki finished typing her train of thought then glanced up. Upon seeing Chloe, her irises contracted in surprise, but the rest of her body kept its cool.

"Hello. I believe we had the pleasure of meeting last night," Chloe said stepping into the room. Her voice and demeanor, all business.

"I'm sorry, I don't..."

"There's no use lying Ms. ... Hot Lips. I followed you home last night."

Vikki lifted a brow, visibly impressed that she had been bested at her own game.

"I see."

"I'm here for two reasons," Chloe continued, taking a seat in front of Vikki's desk. "First, I'd like to know why you felt the need to talk to me in disguise last night."

Vikki stared at her for a moment, her elbows on the arms of her chair, her hands clasped in such a way that all ten of her ruby red, perfectly-manicured fingernails were visible.

"Straight to the point," Vikki replied with a measured grin. "I like that. And I'll do you the courtesy of not beating around the bush either."

Vikki rolled her chair to the side and extracted a manila folder from a top desk drawer.

"Last night, when you let me think Ian was your

beau, I wasn't sure if it was because he's actually a client of yours and you wanted to protect his privacy; or because the two of you really were on a first date."

Vikki pulled out a printout and handed it to Chloe. "Either way... I hate to be the bearer of shitty news, but Ian isn't who you think he is."

Chloe frowned. *What on Earth was she talking about?*

She took the printout in hand and was stunned to see a photo of Ian next to the headline: Ian King, Senior Investigative Reporter.

Chloe quickly discerned she was looking at a photocopy of a biography page on *Veritas Magazine's* website. According to his bio, Ian was a Pulitzer-prize winning journalist with a degree in political science... not architecture.

Chloe cleared her throat. "So you're doing a story on how I'm being hoodwinked by an undercover reporter?"

Vikki shook her head. "Well, that wouldn't be much of a story, actually. Truth is, Ian rarely goes undercover, so I was curious as to why he felt the need to do so with you. Plus, I wanted to speak with you myself, face-to-face, so I could form my own opinion."

Why were journalists so interested in her all of a sudden? Was it all because of Brad Maylis? If so, she never imagined taking him on as a client would cause her this much grief and unwanted publicity.

"So you know Ian?" Chloe asked.

Vikki nodded. "We used to work together a few years back."

Of course you did, Chloe thought as the melody to *It's a Small World* began to play in her head.

"Well, thank you for telling me the truth," she said softly, handing the printout back to Vikki.

"For what it's worth, I wouldn't beat yourself up about this. Ian's very charming, very ambitious and he's *very* good at what he does..."

Chloe closed her eyes as a wave of anger suddenly washed over her, deafening her to the rest of Vikki's words.

She *could not believe* she had been so naive and so trusting as to let a wolf into her inner circle. A wolf who likely meant her harm and global embarrassment, for he had been covertly investigating her for weeks... as though she was in the same league as the human traffickers and corrupt politicians he usually exposed.

According to his bio, Ian was a modern-day crusader against the evils of mankind. Armed with a pen mightier than 10,000 men, he was expert at bringing that which was in the dark – corruption, fraud and other nefarious acts and shadowy enterprises – into the bright lights of the court of public opinion.

For the life of her, Chloe could not fathom why Ian had felt the need to go undercover with her in the first place. What on Earth did he think she was guilty of? And what, pray tell, was his end game?

For his ruse had been elaborate, well-researched and well-planned. Knowing that she worked by referral only, he had feigned a relationship with F. Scott Harrington, a former client of hers.

Knowing that she liked to shadow her clients at work, he had commandeered an all-access pass to an actual construction site; and had roped in friends – or actors, perhaps – like Fitz and Yuri to add an air of authenticity.

And for some inexplicable reason, he had feigned a romantic interest in her, with a script so heartfelt, so eloquent, she had fallen for it hook, line and sinker.

"But, like I said, I've been doing my homework on you," came the sound of Vikki's voice as the deafening wave began to subside, "and you seem to be on the up-and-up. Plus, I've been doing this long enough, I can smell a fraud a mile away. Which is why I wanted to talk to you one-on-one last night. To put a voice to the name; to form my own impression of you."

Vikki slid the printout into the manila folder and returned the folder to its dark abode.

"So, to answer your question, no, I'm not working on another story about you... unless and until I find out you've landed another celebrity client, then all bets are off," Vikki said with a grin that was playful and sincere.

Chloe breathed a quiet sigh. She supposed she should be grateful for small miracles.

"So what's the second thing you wanted to ask me?" Vikki asked.

"Oh, I um... I don't remember," Chloe replied, instinctually.

She always, always, always felt duty bound to bring wandering soulmates together... until now.

All of her matches had been good, thoughtful, upstanding people at heart, which was a prerequisite for a loving and long-lasting relationship.

Knowing what she now knew about Ian, that he had been lying to her for weeks, she had *no idea* who she would be saddling Vikki with if she brought the pair together.

Would it be the charming, witty and thoughtful Ian she thought she had come to know?

Or the wolf in architect's clothing who had no qualms about lying and deceiving his way into getting what he wanted, no matter the personal cost to others?

Until she had a definitive answer to that question, she was at an impasse as to how she wanted to proceed.

So with a handshake and a smile, she departed from Vikki's office, leaving the gossip columnist none the wiser that true love was close – so very, very, *very* close – within her grasp.

Ian sat at his desk, teeth clenched, eyes squeezed

shut as he resisted the urge to *rip his eardrums out.* He was being held hostage by the torturous sound of Muzak, waiting with waning patience for the deputy secretary of the U.S. Department of Health and Human Services to jump on the line.

As the music switched to another god-awful melody, Ian opened his eyes and was surprised to see Pete high-tailing it towards him. For a brief moment, Ian feared a deadly disaster had just befallen the City, for all color had drained from Pete's face.

"What's wrong?" Ian asked.

"Um... so..." Pete stuttered, his voice low. "Chloe's here."

Ian furrowed his brow as he jogged through his mental rolodex of past informants and whistleblowers, for one who may have gone by the code name, Chloe.

"Chloe Daniels," Pete said, filling the void. "The matchmaker. Your matchmaker."

Ian's heart froze. *Oh shit.*

"She's here? At *Veritas?*"

Pete nodded.

"You sure it's her?"

"I'm the one who snagged photos of her, remember," Pete replied.

Shi-iiiit.

Ian shot out of his chair, his mind racing. Chloe was here, which meant she knew he worked here. Which meant that some how, some way, she had found out about him before he had gotten a chance to tell her the truth. Which was precisely what he had planned to do at the close of their date, if she had not bolted out, in chase of someone's soulmate the night before.

"Where is she?" he asked, glancing over Pete's shoulder.

"Well, she was at the front door. I happened to be walking by when she rang the buzzer. But she said she'd be outside waiting for you, in the park across the street."

Ian blanched. Yesterday had been one of the best days he had had in a good long while. Now today was shaping up to be *The Worst*.

He raced out of the office and down the staircase to the first floor, his mind in overdrive.

How had she found out about him and *Veritas*? And how pissed was she? Irreparably so? Or could he, with enough begging and groveling and *mea culpas*, convince her to forgive him and give him another chance... and a thousand lifetimes to make it up to her.

He stepped out of the building and onto the sidewalk. Then he walked to the end of the block and crossed the street to a dog park that was fairly empty at the moment. He spotted Chloe in the distance and was surprised to see her wearing a monochromatic pants suit and heels, her hair pulled back into a wispy bun.

The expression on her face was one he had never seen before: *she was livid.*

"Hey," he said upon approach.

"Hello," she replied with nary a trace of her usual good cheer.

"Before you say anything..." he said, taking an apprehensive step forward.

She stared at him, saying nothing, and the pain and hurt he saw in her eyes damn near broke him in two.

"I had every intention of telling you the truth last night, at the end of our date," he said. "I just... I wanted you to see how things could be between us before I did."

The corner of her lips tightened.

"I take it you're working on a story about me…" she said, her voice monotone.

"I was. It was my editor's idea. He wanted me to do a story on the matchmaking business. He thought it would help me get over the breakup with Meaghan," he said. "When I signed on as your client, I did so with a lot of skeptical assumptions about you; about matchmakers in general. But the more time we spent together and the more I got to know you, the more I wanted to know you. And for you to know me, the real me."

"And your story?" she asked.

"Dead. DOA. Last week, I told my editor I didn't have anything to go on and I was able to sell him on a different story instead."

"I see," she said, her face pensive.

Ian had expected Gunderson to be furious that he wanted to kill the matchmaker story weeks after the magazine had spent a pretty penny on Chloe's retainer fee. But surprisingly, Gunderson had taken the news in stride:

"I've got the old Ian back," he had said, referring to the string of fiery pieces – with plenty of *sparkle* – Ian had been writing of late. "As far as I'm concerned, it was money well spent."

Ian noticed that Chloe's shoulders had relaxed a bit upon learning he had not, and would not, be publishing a story on her or her business.

"When I asked you out," he said, taking another step forward, "it was on impulse. A pure and honest impulse. Everything I said to you the other night, about how I feel and what I believe, I meant every word. The only thing I've lied to you about was my last name and my occupation. Oh, and I've never been to a WNBA game in my life. But everything else has been the truth."

"What about Fitz?" she asked.

"He really is an architect and my best friend since pre-school."

"Meagan and the breakup email?"

He nodded.

"And Celeste? Did you really buy VIP tickets a year ago?"

"I did."

"I see," she said, staring off into the distance, her face solemn.

Ian took another step forward. "I really believe the universe or destiny or whatever, brought us together for a reason and I feel…"

"Fate did bring us together," she interjected. "But not for the reason you think."

She shifted her gaze and looked him straight in the eye. "I'm not your soulmate, Ian," she said softly, steadily.

"Don't say that," he said, reaching for her hands, as if the act of intertwining his fingers with hers would keep him from losing her. "Be angry with me. Slap me, yell at me, but please don't say that."

He gazed into her eyes and was surprised to find that now, instead of pain, they were filled with angelic calm.

"It's the truth. I know I'm not your soulmate, because I know the woman who is."

He blinked. "What?"

"I saw her last night, in the restaurant. That's why I left so abruptly."

He stared at her, slack-jawed.

"You're serious?"

"I am."

"You're not saying this because you're angry with me? For lying to you? Deceiving you?"

She shook her head. "I'm not angry with you anymore, Ian."

"Just like that?"

She nodded. "I believe you."

He blinked with disbelief, amazed by the lightning speed with which she had let go of her anger and disdain. This definitely gave new meaning to the dictum: *The truth will set you free.*

"You know, sometimes you're too incredible to be true," he whispered.

"Like you said, Fate brought us together for a reason. If we had not gone to Pampas last night, and if you had not been doing an undercover story on me, then I would not have seen your soulmate. I only hope that, based on the time we've spent together, you trust me enough to agree to meet her in person."

Ian groaned and ran a frustrated hand through his hair. This was *not at all* how he had expected this day or this conversation to go.

He moved to a nearby bench and sat, feeling as though the wind had been knocked out of him. He stared blankly at the ground.

"I don't understand how this..." he said, his voice barely a whisper. "These feelings I have for you, they are very real."

"I know," she said, sitting next to him. "But feelings, they can come and they can go."

She placed a comforting hand on his knee.

"True love, however, lasts forever. And right now, at this very moment, true love is within your grasp. All you have to do is say yes."

His gaze remained frozen on the ground for a long moment. Then he squeezed his eyes shut, wanting, not wanting to ask...

"Who is she?"

"I can't tell you, but I can show you," Chloe replied. "I'll arrange a time and a place for you to meet each other in person. All I'll say in the meantime is, she's sugar *and* spice. Beautiful, astute, kind-hearted and... *perfect for you.*"

She stood up and gazed down at him with a sparkle in her eye and a smile on her lips.

"Think about it and let me know. You know how to reach me."

He watched her walk away, his head spinning, his heart a jumble of emotions, as four simple words echoed in his ears.

True love lasts forever.

FIFTEEN

A week and a half later, Chloe stood at the foot of a cobblestone path leading up to an expansive conservatory.

She watched as a male peacock pranced across the manicured lawn in front of her, a train of gorgeous feathers gliding behind him. All about her was an Eden of flowering trees, babbling brooks and the cool rays of the morning sun.

Chloe had a special love for this place, a private botanical garden on Long Island that was peaceful, quaint and wondrously romantic. She only used it when matching up couples for whom privacy from paparazzi and the public eye was paramount.

This was where Brad and Lia had first laid eyes on one another.

And, hopefully, this would be where Vikki and Ian would begin their journey of love, marriage and baby carriages.

Her phone buzzed. She answered it without looking at the caller ID.

"Hello?"

"Hey Chloe, your second guest just arrived. Cool to let him in?"

Oh, thank baby Cupid! Chloe thought, breathing a huge sigh of relief.

A small part of her had feared Ian would wake up that morning with skittishly cold feet and end up being a no-show. Sometimes the hardest part of her job was getting both parties to show up. Everything else from there on out was a breeze.

"Yes, Freddie. Thanks," she replied.

"Anytime."

The garden boasted two gated and guarded entrances, which was especially useful on days like this wherein she could direct each soulmate to arrive at staggered times and different gates. She normally spaced them about fifteen minutes apart. And the guards always called her before granting them entrée, to ensure neither soulmate ended up running into the other prematurely.

She wanted their rendezvous to be as intimate and romantic as possible.

After her tough conversation with Ian days before, and after he had finally agreed to meet his soulmate in person, she had circled back with Vikki, who had been skeptical yet intrigued when Chloe shared that she knew someone who was *perfect* for her.

Chloe imagined that, in the battle between Vikki's innate curiosity and her journalistic skepticism, curiosity had won out in the end.

Chloe also intuited that the dating game was, no doubt, especially hard for a woman like Vikki. Most men would find her IQ, her feminism, her looks, or the whole witty, vivacious and strong-willed package incredibly intimidating. And the remaining few could probably be divided into men who were only interested in seeing her in bed; men who wanted the prestige of dating a semi-celebrity; and a teeny-teeny-tiny subset of men who were interested in getting to know the real woman behind the Vikki Hot Lips brand.

Chloe knew Ian was smart, mature and confident

enough to cherish a woman like Vikki. And, underneath the ruby red lipstick and va-va-voom persona, Vikki was the kind, adventurous and down-to-Earth woman Ian desired.

Vikki had arrived ten minutes before, her aura calm yet apprehensive.

Chloe had greeted her with a warm hug and a reassuring smile. Then she escorted Vikki inside the conservatory to a stone bench, where she left her in wait of her soulmate – like a modern-day Juliet.

The same reassuring smile spread across Chloe's face when Ian rounded a bend and came into view. He looked tired and nervous, as if he still was not sure he wanted to go through with this.

Chloe was just grateful he had shown up. To her that meant that, subconsciously, he was definitely ready and eager to fall in love with his soulmate.

Their client-matchmaker relationship may have started out under false pretenses, but the end result would be exactly what Ian had been craving for far too long.

"Hey," she said, giving him a warm hug. "Happy Sunday!"

"Happy Sunday," he said, his voice bereft of emotion.

"So... are you ready to meet your soulmate?"

He gazed down at her, his eyes forlorn. She could tell he was holding on to doubt simply because of his lingering feelings for her.

"Are you sure about this?" he asked.

"One hundred percent," she replied.

Ian breathed a deep, long sigh as Chloe escorted him to the glass doors of the conservatory, which were frosted with moisture from the humidity inside.

"She's waiting for you by the orchids," she said with an angelic grin as she opened one of the doors, inviting him to step inside...

Ian squared his shoulders and crossed over the threshold into the conservatory's warm embrace. Chloe closed the door behind him, leaving him alone in a foreign land where *eau de fleurs* hung heady in the air.

He began to walk down a cobblestone path that meandered through verdant cocoons of exotic flowers, trees and vines hailing from jungles and rainforests throughout the Southern Hemisphere.

As he drew nigh to the rear of the conservatory, he rounded a corner and saw a woman standing before a wall of orchids.

Though her back was to him, he recognized her immediately.

It was Vikki, out of disguise. Her hair was pulled back in a simple ponytail and she was clad in jeans, a boat neck top and high-heeled sandals.

"Vikki," he breathed as he wrapped his mind around the revelation that Victoria Marie Gjrnovic, a woman he had known for over a decade, was his soulmate.

Vikki turned at the sound of his voice and stared back at him, stunned.

"Ian.... What are you doing here?"

He thought about the few occasions he had been tempted to ask her out but never followed through – convincing himself that dating a co-worker was too risky a proposition. Then, years later, when he had moved to *Veritas*, convincing himself that the newly reinvented Vikki Hot Lips was way too high maintenance for his taste.

"The same reason you're here," he replied.

Vikki's lips, which were glossed a pale pink instead of her signature ruby red, dipped into a frown. "I'm afraid a cruel joke is being played on us."

"Why would you say that?"

"Chloe knows who you really are, and that you've been deceiving her for weeks."

Ian could feel the pit of guilt still toiling in his stomach. Chloe may have forgiven him, but he was not quite ready to absolve himself just yet. He hated that he had caused her any pain or sadness.

"I know," he said, solemnly.

"She told you?"

He nodded.

"Did she tell you I was the one who told her?"

Ian blinked with surprise. "No."

"So she didn't tell you about the other night?"

He shook his head.

"When I saw you at the children's hospital press event, I had a sneaking suspicion you were working on something related to Chloe and Maylis, so I had one of my PIs follow you."

Ian's eyes smiled. Of course Vikki had private investigators on retainer.

"I wasn't sure what you were up to, but I figured

that if you had gone undercover, you must be working on something big, something I'd missed. So last weekend, I donned one of my disguises and shadowed the two of you to that backyard comedy club, then the restaurant. When Chloe went to the ladies room, I followed her, struck up a conversation and discovered that the two of you were, supposedly, on some kind of date. Then I left the restaurant, went home and, to my surprise, the next morning, Chloe Daniels materializes in front of my desk, demanding to know why I had been following her in disguise."

Ian pursed his lips. *So that explained how Chloe had seen the two of them in close proximity.*

"So," Vikki continued. "Seeing how both of us have a history of deceiving her in the interest of a story, I imagine this is her way of getting back at us."

He shook his head. "She's not like that."

Vikki gave him a look. "Everyone's like that."

"She's not."

Vikki furrowed her brow and stared at him for a long moment. "So you believe her? You believe her when she says we're soulmates?"

Ian was struck by how quickly and easily his feelings for Chloe and Meaghan and all the other women in his past faded away as he gazed upon the woman he was destined have and to hold for the rest of his life.

Feelings come and go. True love lasts forever.

"I do," he said, softly, taking a few steps towards her.

"Are you willing to bet your Pulitzer on that belief?" she asked, nervously clutching the strap of her purse.

"I am."

She gazed into his eyes. "You're serious," she whispered.

He nodded, stepping into her orbit and closing the distance between them.

Ian watched as her lashes, free from extensions or mascara, slowly fell to the floor, shielding her eyes from his gaze. "You know, I've always had a thing for you. But you never seemed interested," she said, her voice shy.

"I was always interested. I just... never acted on it. Something I'm really starting to regret right now."

"Why didn't you?" she asked.

"Because..." he said, searching for the just-right word. But all he could come up with was...

"I'm an idiot."

Vikki giggled.

Ian took her hands in his. "I can't believe you've been right in front of me all this time."

Vikki's lashes lifted. Their eyes locked.

"Kiss me," she said simply, as if she needed more than just words to absolve her fears and her doubts.

Ian reached up to caress her cheek. Her eyes shuttered at the feel of his skin against her own. He brushed his thumb across the blush of her lips. They were soft and warm and irresistibly inviting.

Long gone were thoughts of kissing Chloe or any other woman for that matter. All he wanted in that moment was the *hot lips* of Victoria Gjrnovic, his soulmate.

He leaned in close, intoxicated by her scent, amazed that this was the woman he was destined to spend his life with.

Then he tilted his head just so and kissed her, just as she had commanded.

As their kiss deepened, he wrapped his arms around her waist and pulled her in close. And for the first time in his life, he found in that kiss something he had never felt with any of the women who had come before.

He felt at home.

SIXTEEN

Chloe stood in front of her bedroom closet, arms crossed, her head cocked to the side as she stared at a color-coordinated wave of clothes.

"So how'd it go with Mr. *Liar Liar Pants on Fire?*" Jenna asked, waltzing in, having just returned from a private viewing of Lascada's collection-in-progress for New York Fashion Week.

Chloe grabbed her cell phone, unlocked it and showed Jenna a text message Ian had sent hours before. In it was a photo of him and Vikki, both smiling cheek-to-cheek in front of a wall of orchids, accompanied with two simple words: *Thank You!*

Jenna's left brow shot up. "That's Vikki Hot Lips?"

Chloe nodded.

"Wow, she looks... nice... and normal."

Chloe chuckled. "She is. When she's in work mode, she's no nonsense and a force of nature. But deep down, she's a sweetheart."

"Who knew?" Jenna's eyes shifted to Ian's mug in the photo. "But Mr. *I'm-Not-An-Actual-Architect* is still persona non-grata in my book."

Chloe's face grew pensive. "You know, while I don't condone Ian's actions, I forgive them. I don't think he would've believed me when I showed him Vikki was his soulmate if we had not spent all that time together. Journalists are a skeptical lot."

"Chloe Daniels... forever the kind-hearted optimist. Well, I suppose I'm glad he found happiness."

Jenna glanced down and spotted a suitcase leaning on the side of Chloe's bed. "Going somewhere?"

Chloe sighed. "Yeah, I just need to get away for a bit."

Jenna sat on the edge of the bed. "Where to?"

"Italy."

"Italy!"

Chloe nodded.

"Really? Since when?"

"Since about an hour ago."

"Chloe, are you serious? You're seriously going to Italy?"

She nodded once more.

"By yourself?"

"I've been wanting to go somewhere, anywhere, farther than the Caribbean for forever, and I figure now's as good a time as any."

"Oh my god. *A*, I'm shocked. *B*, I sooooo want to come with you. You can't wait a week or two? I'm sure I can either guilt or sweet talk Manuel into giving me the time off with a bit more lead time."

Chloe frowned and shook her head. "The tickets are nonrefundable. But if you can get the time off, you should meet me over there. It'll be fun!"

"Wait, how long are you going for?"

"Two weeks. Maybe three."

"You minx," Jenna said with a grin of approval. "Well you deserve it, after the crazy weeks you've had."

Chloe chuckled. "Tell me about it."

The next morning, Chloe's heart skipped a beat as her taxi slowed to a stop in front of JFK's international terminal.

She was going to Italy! She was actually going to Italy!

She hopped out the cab and took in the hustle and bustle of travelers hailing from all corners of the globe. She gave the driver a generous tip then sailed through a pair of sliding doors, wheeling a carry-on suitcase behind her.

With a mobile ticket in hand, she beelined straight to the security line, which was long but not crazy long, thankfully enough.

Though her demeanor was bright-eyed and bushy-tailed, inside she was an avalanche of nerves. This would be her first time traveling overseas *hans solo* and she had *no idea* what she was getting herself into. Nothing had been planned beyond her flight and first few nights in a Roman hotel. She was hoping to map out more of a game plan whilst cruising over the Atlantic, assuming she did not conk out shortly after takeoff, since last-minute packing had kept her from getting a good night's rest the night before.

Once she made it through security with nary a beep or 'Excuse me miss, we need to inspect your bag,' Chloe detoured into duty-free to buy a super comfy travel pillow and a much-needed travel guide to Italy. Then she began the long walk to her gate at the end of the terminal.

Beams of sunlight streamed through an orchestra of windows. Chloe squinted her eyes against the blinding light and mentally checked to make sure she had packed her favorite pair of sunglasses.

In the distance, her eyes were drawn to the shape and body of a man who was tall and well-dressed. Due to the sun's glare, she could not make out his face; but she was pretty sure he had just diverted from his path and was moving diagonally across the wide and busy walkway, straight towards her.

"Now this is a homecoming I definitely wasn't expecting," came the tenor of a voice she would recognize anywhere.

"Oh my goodness," Chloe said, stopping in her tracks. She turned her back to the sun-soaked windows and her irises focused in on Alexander's face, which was just as surprised to see her as she was to see him.

He looked debonair as always. So much so, one

would find it hard to believe he had just stepped off a long, international flight.

"Welcome back to the USA," she said.

"Well, I *would* be glad to be back, but I get the distinct impression you're about to leave me," he replied, glancing at her suitcase. "Where are you headed?"

"Rome."

"Really? For work?"

"For fun. I'm *finally* taking a long awaited and much-needed vacation."

He slid a hand into his pants pocket. "How long has this been in the works?"

"Since yesterday."

His brows shot up. "Really?"

"A flight of temporary insanity, perhaps."

"Not at all. How long will you be gone?"

"Two or three weeks?"

"So you'll be city hopping, I presume?"

"Yeah, I'm thinking of doing Rome then Florence and Venice and maybe Naples or Paris. Kind of just playing it by ear."

His eyes smiled. "That's the way to do it. Is Jenna coming with you?"

"She's going to try to meet me next weekend, if she can get the time off."

"Well I'm glad I ran into you before you disappeared on me again," he teased.

"This time around, I won't change my phone number, promise."

He chuckled. "I have a cousin, Valentina, who lives in Rome; and an aunt and uncle in Venice. I'll see if they're in town and can show you around. My aunt loves to cook and all she asks in return is that you love to eat."

"Oh my goodness! That would be amazing. Thank you."

He took out his wallet, handed her a card. "Call me at this number when you've settled into your hotel. It's toll free."

"Will do."

"Well, *buon viaggio*," he said with a grin. "I hope you enjoy every second of your trip. But one piece of advice…"

"What's that?"

"Don't fall in love with an Italian while you're there."

Chloe furrowed her brow. "Why not?"

"Because..." he said, his voice low and serious. "I haven't taken you on an official first date, yet."

Chloe stared at him, stunned into stillness. *Did he just say what she thought he just said?*

Alexander leaned in close and gave her a parting kiss to the cheek.

"*Ciao, bella,*" he said with that sexy grin of his as he turned and walked away.

Chloe stared after him, slowly trying to process *what had just happened.*

So it turned out Alexander was not interested in just being brunch-buddies after all.

More enlightening than that was the way her heart was beating all of a sudden.

Because I haven't taken you on an official first date, yet.

The depth of feeling behind those words had set her heart aflutter. And, surprisingly enough, for the first time ever in the long course of their friendship, she welcomed the sensation.

Chloe still had no idea if Alexander was her soulmate or not, but over the past few weeks, she had rediscovered a truism that had lain dormant within her for years:

Life is much more interesting and fulfilling when one is willing to take a leap of faith.

She had taken a leap of faith with Greg and, more recently, with Ian. Though neither of them had led to happily-ever-after, she had zero regrets. She got to share three fun and exciting years with Greg; and she had the honor and pleasure of pairing Ian with his one true love.

She had also taken a leap of faith when she quit her job to do matchmaking full-time. And in the years since, she had never been happier.

Whether a leap of faith with Alexander would lead to something short-term or long-term, she was looking forward to taking their friendship to the next level upon her return. She had it on good authority, from one of his exes, that Alexander was an *amazing* kisser.

Chloe continued on to her gate, floating on a cloud of excitement. Not just because of Alexander's unmistakable declaration of interest, but also because, in the blink of an eye, she had gone from having zero plans to having two potential opportunities to experience slices-of-life in Italy that most tourists were not privy to. Oh, how lovely it would be to enjoy a home-cooked meal in Venice;

or a Roman night on the town with Alexander's posh cousin... for how could she not be fashionably posh with a name like Valentina!

At the gate, Chloe settled into a chair by the windows and gazed out at the tarmac, in awe of the modern innovations that made international air travel possible. She could not believe that ten hours from now, she would be in Rome!

She pulled out the travel guide and began to read, dog-earring pages with places of interest along the way.

"Passengers Marc La Pierre, Chloe Daniels and Ashe Shaheedi, can you please come to Gate B64 to speak with an agent? Thank you."

Chloe looked up from the guide. *Had they just said her name? And if so, why?*

She made her way to the gate desk where she spoke with a lovely young woman named Charisma, who had the unenviable task of being the bearer of bad news.

"Ms. Daniels, I'm sorry to have to inform you the flight is overbooked. And, because you purchased your ticket just last night, we're going to have to put you on standby. I will do everything I can to get you on this flight but, barring that, I already have a guaranteed seat reserved for you on the next one."

"O-kay," Chloe replied, feeling a bit deflated, as if Charisma had just taken a bite out of her Cloud 9. "What time does that flight leave?"

"Midnight. Tonight."

Chloe's face blanched. *Midnight? That's half a day from now.*

"I know this is a bit frustrating. But I will definitely do what I can to get you on this flight," Charisma said in earnest.

"Okay, thanks," Chloe replied, retreating back to her seat.

For a brief moment, she was tempted to hop into a cab and return to the comfort of her bed rather than wait around in hopes of getting onto a flight that was clearly overbooked, given the number of people milling about the gate. But, then, she figured it would be best to just sit in the coolness of the airport rather than a taxi that would be mired in rush hour traffic for over an hour each way. Luckily, she had her tablet, access to wifi and a nearby electrical outlet. She could wile the hours away by catching up on her favorite TV shows.

When the boarding process began, Chloe leaned

back in her seat, willing herself to relax. She glanced at Charisma, who was standing by the door to the gate, scanning one ticket after another. Then she cued up some classical Puccini on her iPad, closed her eyes and pictured herself ascending ancient steps in the Roman Coliseum; savoring a bottle of Chianti in Tuscany; kayaking along the Grand Canal in Venice.

Whether her flight took off that day or the next... or the next, she was still headed to Italy, the cradle of the Roman empire. And that was enough to make her smile.

Moments later, Chloe felt a light tap on her shoulder and drifted back to reality. She opened her eyes and saw Charisma smiling down at her.

"Hi, Ms. Daniels," she said.

Chloe slid the audio buds from her ears.

"I've got some bad news and good news. The bad news is, our coach cabin is completely full."

Chloe gave a slow nod.

"The good news is, you've been upgraded to our first class lounge on this flight, at no extra charge."

Chloe starred at her dumbfounded. "Are you serious?"

Charisma grinned. "I hope that will be acceptable."

Chloe looked up at the heavens, silently thanking Fate for such unexpected good fortune.

"Oh my goodness, thank you Charisma. I really appreciate it."

"My pleasure."

Chloe followed her to the door to the jetway, where Charisma handed her a freshly-printed ticket. She looked down and took stock of her new seat number: 2A.

As she walked down the jetway to the plane, she glanced up towards the heavens once more and grinned. Now there was nary a doubt in her mind that zipping off to Italy was *precisely* what she should be doing right now.

She exchanged greetings with a flight attendant as she stepped aboard, then she turned to her left to enter the first class cabin. As she did so, her eyes immediately glanced to the right. The second row was occupied by an Italian couple in their forties, both chicly dressed in tight jeans and designer tops.

Then she glanced to her left and was stunned into stillness.

She blinked.

Then blinked again.

Then blinked once more to ensure her eyes were not deceiving her.

Sure enough, in the seat next to hers sat a man who looked very much like Alexander Turin, smiling at her in that intoxicating way of his, although Chloe noticed there was a hint of nervousness in his gaze.

"Hey," he said, standing.

"What are you...?"

"Ladies and gentlemen, welcome aboard," a flight attendant chirped over the intercom. Alexander reached for Chloe's carry-on and, with unsurprising ease and grace, nestled it in the storage compartment above.

"We will be pulling away from the gate momentarily. Please be seated and make sure your personal belongings are secure, your tray tables are stowed and your seats are in an upright position."

Chloe took her seat by the window as the flight attendant switched to Italian. Alexander sat down beside her, buckled his seatbelt then met her stare.

"I hope you don't mind, I've decided to Bogart your trip."

"You're Bogarting my trip?" she parroted, still a little stunned.

"I'd like to volunteer myself as your personal tour guide," he said, gazing at her with naked vulnerability. "I hope that's okay."

"But what about work?" she asked.

"Like you, I'm long past due for a vacation. Plus, I have a global phone and they have pretty good wifi in Italy, so if someone needs to reach me, they can reach me. Not to mention, I'm a partner now, so they can't really fire me or anything."

She shook her head. "I can't believe you just bought a plane ticket like that."

Then realization dawned on her face. "Did they really comp me up to first-class or did you buy my ticket?"

His eyes twinkled as he leaned the side of his head on the headrest. "You know, my entire flight home, I was antsy because I couldn't wait to see you."

For a split second, Chloe lost the ability to think or breathe.

"Then I get to see you sooner than expected, only to find out you're leaving the country. I just thank my lucky stars I ran into you when I did." He took her hand in his. "But since I'm a gentleman, I'll only Bogart your trip with your permission. You're well within your right to tell me to get lost when we land in Rome."

She was struck by how much the feel of him, his skin on her skin, was affecting her like never before. He was so handsome and magnetic and obviously a romantic given this grand gesture of his – to jet right back across the ocean on a whim, just to be with her.

He was everything she could have ever dreamed of. And that dream, which had frightened her for years, was now the very thing she wanted most.

She really wanted to be in this dream with him... whether it lasted for a week or twelve or longer.

"I suppose it wouldn't hurt to have my own personal tour guide who speaks fluent Italian," she said with a grin.

He gazed at her in the way da Vinci surely must have gazed upon Mona Lisa.

"I'm fully and completely at your service, *signorina*."

"*Grazie*," she said, using one of the few Italian words she actually did know. She had planned to learn a few more during the flight.

"I do have a confession to make, though," he said. "I have an ulterior motive for Bogarting your trip."

"What's that?"

He leaned in close, his gorgeous eyes shimmering into hers.

"It's because I want our first kiss to be in Venice, on the Rialto Bridge, under the moonlight."

He lifted her hand to his lips and kissed the soft curve of her fingers.

"If you're amenable, of course," he added.

A slow, dreamy smile spread across Chloe's face as she lost herself in the heart, soul and heat of Alexander's gaze.

She couldn't wait to get to Venice!

XOXO

Dearest reader,

I hope you enjoyed this tale and fell in love with the magic of love as much as I did!

Want to be the first to know when my next novel debuts? Visit tbpearl.com to join my email list.

With love,

t.b.pearl

p.s., Would you kindly take a moment to post a review for *A Match Made By Chloe* on Amazon, Goodreads, et. al.? Thanks much for sharing the love!